MYSTERY AT OLYMPIA

John Rhode was a pseudonym for the author Cecil Street (1884–1964), who also wrote as Miles Burton and Cecil Waye. Having served in the British Army as an artillery officer during the First World War, rising to the rank of Major, he began writing non-fiction before turning to detective fiction, and produced four novels a year for thirty-seven years.

As his list of detective stories grew, so did the public's appetite for his particular blending of humdrum everyday life with the startling appearance of the most curious kind of crimes. It was the *Sunday Times* who said of John Rhode that 'he must hold the record for the invention of ingenious forms of murder', and the *Times Literary Supplement* described him as 'standing in the front rank of those who write detective fiction'.

Rhode's first series novel, *The Paddington Mystery* (1925), introduced Dr Lancelot Priestley, who went on to appear in 72 novels, many of them for Collins Crime Club. The Priestley books are classics of scientific detection, with the elderly Dr Priestley demonstrating how apparently impossible crimes have been carried out, and they are now highly sought after by collectors.

By the same author

Death at Breakfast
Invisible Weapons

JOHN RHODE

Mystery at Olympia

COLLINS
CRIME
CLUB

COLLINS CRIME CLUB

An imprint of HarperCollins*Publishers*
1 London Bridge Street
London SE1 9GF
www.harpercollins.co.uk

This paperback edition 2018

First published in Great Britain by Collins Crime Club 1935

A catalogue record for this book is available from the British Library

ISBN 978-0-00-826878-7

Typeset in Sabon by Palimpsest Book Production Ltd, Falkirk, Stirlingshire

Printed and bound in Great Britain
by CPI Group (UK) Ltd, Croydon CR0 4YY

MIX
Paper from
responsible sources
FSC™ C007454

This book is produced from independently certified FSC™ paper
to ensure responsible forest management.

For more information visit: www.harpercollins.co.uk/green

CHAPTER I

The directors of the Comet Motor Car Company have always been remarkable for their boldness and foresight. By their adoption of new ideas, while their competitors were still mistrustful of the innovation, they have always managed to keep Comet cars just a little more up-to-date than the latest models produced by their rivals. But their acquisition of the patent rights in the Lovell Transmission, and the application of that ingenious invention to all their cars, from the largest to the smallest, provided a sensation which will not readily be forgotten by the motoring public.

To that public the appearance of the Lovell Transmission was of dramatic suddenness. Nobody outside the Comet works at Coventry knew of the months of research and experiment carried on behind locked doors. The young inventor himself, Charles Lovell, had worked night and day almost without intermission. It was said that he had to be forcibly removed from the test-bench before he would consent to take a hurried meal. And it is quite certain that during the final stages he slept in a hammock slung up at one end of the machine-shop.

But the secret was jealously guarded. Not until a week before the Olympia Motor Show was a single word allowed to leak out. And then the advertising agency which dealt with the propaganda of the Comet Motor Car Company was given its head. In every newspaper and periodical the advertisement appeared. It was announced that in future Comet cars would have no gear-box, no clutch, no radiator, and no self-starter, since all these had been rendered unnecessary by the adoption of the Lovell Transmission. No further information was vouchsafed, but the advertisements concluded with the invitation, printed in large type, 'Come and see them on Stand 1001 at Olympia!'

This was provocative, as it was meant to be. The exhibition cars, swathed in tarpaulins, were brought to Olympia in furniture vans, each guarded by half a dozen of the firm's employees. Still with the tarpaulins enveloping them, they were wheeled on to the stand, where their devoted guards kept an eagle-eyed watch. Not until five minutes before the show opened were the tarpaulins removed and the mysteries which they had hitherto concealed laid bare.

Stand 1001 was situated almost in the centre of the vast building. And, from the very moment when the public were admitted on the first day of the show, it became the focus of the vast crowds who paid for admittance, and perhaps even more of those that did not. The general public were inquisitive. Their curiosity had been aroused, and, like the Athenians of old, they were eager to hear or to tell of some new thing. But to the journalists, the dealers, the designers of competing makes, all those professionally concerned in the industry, the situation was agonising. To obtain information about this new move on the part of the Comet people was vital to their bread and butter.

The consequence was that during the whole duration of the show it needed the exercise of patience and perseverance to get within sight of Stand 1001. Actually to get on to it, to obtain a close view of one of the new models, might take, under the most favourable conditions, an hour or more. From ten in the morning till ten at night a closely packed throng, men and women, young and old, surged round the stand, upon which half a dozen alert young salesmen were kept busy in explaining to successive batches of visitors the advantages of the new system.

This was, of course, excellent publicity from the Comet people's point of view. But it had its disadvantages. On the very first day of the show it was found impossible to conduct any business whatever on the overcrowded stand. Every inch of space was invaded by people anxious to see. Dealers wishing to place contracts and individual buyers were extricated from the mob and carried to the London show-rooms by a fleet of cars provided for the purpose. There, in comparative calm, they were enabled to place their orders.

On Monday, October 8th, Doctor Oldland, that prosperous Kensington practitioner, visited the Motor Show. He did so every year, and would not have missed the occasion for the world. He had a mechanical mind, to which the development of the motor car was an unfailing source of interest. But that was by no means the only attraction which the show held for him. He was not at all gregarious, preferring the company of one or two special friends to a larger assembly. But he liked to watch a crowd, to see a vast concourse of human beings obeying the same laws, flowing together in the same slow streams like so many particles of inert matter. Perhaps it satisfied his sardonic ideas upon the general futility of things. However this may be, he usually spent a good part of his time in one of the corners of the gallery, whence he could look down upon the busy scene below.

This year, though, his visit had a more immediate purpose. He had come to the conclusion that it was nearly time he bought a new car. It had taken him a long time to become reconciled to the idea. It was not the expense which had given him pause. He could have afforded a couple or more, had they been necessary. But he hated change, unless it could be proved to him that it brought with it some definite advantage. He had to be convinced, for instance, that a new drug or a new method of treatment were definite improvements upon their predecessors before he could be persuaded to adopt them himself.

Even as he paid for his admission at the turnstile, and mingled with the stream pouring into the great hall, his misgivings returned. There was nothing in the world the matter with his present car. It was only three years old, and still good for years of faithful service. True, his chauffeur had been hinting lately that it was more difficult than it used to be to keep it looking really smart. But what did that matter? Oldland told himself, with one of his queer wry smiles, that it was the same with cars as with men. A man like himself, rising fifty, must necessarily expend more energy on keeping himself smart than a spruce young fellow barely out of his teens. Like his own son Bill, for instance.

Dash it all, why hadn't he got Bill to come down from Yorkshire to go round the stands with him? Bill was an engineer, and knew as much about the insides of motor

4

cars as his father did of the insides of humans. Bill would be sympathetic, perhaps even enthusiastic, whatever make the old man decided upon. They were far too good friends ever to adopt an attitude of superiority to one another. But would Bill be able to refrain from saying, 'I wish I'd known you were going to buy a new car, Dad! I could have put you on to something . . .'

With a short laugh, Oldland put these forebodings aside. He had come to the show to order a new car, and he was not going home until the order had been placed. He could not face his chauffeur, waiting outside with the old car, until this had been done. The man was quite right, confound him! A doctor's turnout must be above suspicion of age or decay. It must be bright, new, and sparkling, in order to inspire trust in the breasts of misanthropic patients.

Oldland allowed himself to be carried forward by the stream, glancing without any great interest at the stands as he drifted slowly past them. Hawk-faced salesmen, detecting by some sixth sense a potential buyer, endeavoured to catch his eye. But he was too old a bird to be entangled in that snare. He knew the dangers of listening to the voice of the siren. 'May I show you our new thirty horsepower model, sir? The very last word in luxury and efficiency!' As though luxury could ever be efficient, or efficiency luxurious! The less wary might listen, lulled to their fate by a flow of smooth and seductive verbiage, until, conquered by the mesmeric powers of salesmanship, they placed an order. Not so the experienced Oldland. He would see for himself, and make his own decision.

The stream swept him unresisting towards Stand 1001. The Comet advertisement had not escaped his attention. His first reaction to it had been one of irritation. Why couldn't the confounded people give particulars? What would be thought of a doctor who said, 'I can dispense with drugs and bandages and splints. I'm not going to tell you how. If you want to know, you'll have to come to my surgery and see.' Yet that, in effect, was what these people said.

But his mechanical curiosity struggled with his annoyance, and eventually won the day. He would visit Stand 1001, and see what new-fangled stunt the Comet people had got hold of now. But only to satisfy his own inquisitiveness. Most certainly not with any intention to purchase. The Lovell Transmission might be all right for people who could find no better use for their money than to try out other people's ideas with it. He wanted something that had years of experience on the road behind it.

The stream, of which Oldland was an unconsidered drop, slackened and came to rest as it approached Stand 1001. But it was still early in the afternoon, barely half-past two, and the crowd was not so dense as at other times. Some visitors had gone to lunch, others had not yet arrived from that meal. Oldland patiently edged his way towards the centre of attraction. In less time than he had any right to expect, he found himself standing within a few feet of one of the chassis which had given rise to so much speculation.

Within a few feet of it. By standing on tiptoe, he could manage to catch a glimpse of polished metal. But in between was a serried mass of humanity, so tightly packed together that it was impossible for any single individual to move or turn. Periodically, however, this mass surged and erupted, throwing off perhaps a dozen of its human particles. Others immediately took their places, and the mass coalesced as tightly as before.

Oldland, taking advantage of these periodical eruptions, gradually wormed his way to the front of the mass. Separated from his audience by the width of a stripped chassis, one of the Comet salesmen was explaining the principles of the Lovell Transmission to all who could press within earshot.

'We claim that the control is the simplest that has yet been devised,' he was saying. 'There is, as you can see, no gear lever, since the car has no gears. Nor is there a self-starter button, since the engine is started by a method which I shall hope to explain later. In fact, the only controls are the hand brake lever, and these two pedals which you see, one on either side of the steering column.

'The principle upon which the transmission works is entirely novel. The car is driven, not directly by the engine, but by a turbine, which gives a smoother motion than any reciprocating engine, however many cylinders it might have. This turbine is bolted to the back axle, immediately in front of the differential, thus doing away with the necessity for a long propeller shaft. The space between the turbine and the engine is taken up by this series of steel cylinders.'

The salesman had evidently learnt his lesson well, Oldland thought. If one were to interrupt him by an ill-timed question, he would probably have to begin all over again at the beginning. But none of his audience seemed inclined to ask such a question. All eyes were concentrated upon the various parts of the chassis, as the demonstrator pointed them out.

'The engine drives a pump, of a new and highly efficient type. The inlet side of this pump is connected by this copper pipe of large bore to the exhaust end of the turbine. The delivery side of the pump is connected by this smaller steel pipe to the steel cylinders, which are interconnected. When the car is delivered, these cylinders are full or nearly full, of liquid sulphur dioxide.

'The turbine is driven by this sulphur dioxide. When the connection between the cylinders and the turbine is opened, the liquid vaporises, and produces a rush of gas through the turbine, which revolves, and this drives the car. The gas, after doing its work, goes to the pump, where it is once more liquefied by pressure and returned to the cylinders.

'You will observe that both pump and turbine are jacketted. The compression of the gas in the pump produces heat, and this is utilised in the following way. The pump jacket contains oil, and in this is immersed a carburettor of special design. The mixture, before reaching the engine, is thus heated to such a degree that the petrol is completely vaporised, thus giving ideal combustion in the engine cylinders.

'The turbine jacket is similarly filled with oil. But here the effect produced is exactly the reverse of that of the pump. The vaporisation of the liquid sulphur dioxide produces cold, as in the ordinary refrigerator. The cold oil circulates by means of these pipes to the water-jacket, or rather oil-jacket, of the engine, which is thus kept at a suitable temperature.

'Now I will explain the control, which is simplicity itself. The two pedals are interconnected in such a way that when one is pressed down, the other comes out. A gentle spring is fitted, so that if both feet are removed from the pedals, the right-hand one is fully depressed and, therefore, the left-hand one fully out. This, then, is the normal position of the pedals, as you see them on this chassis. In this position the brakes are fully on. But they can be released by pushing the hand-brake lever forward, should it be necessary to move the car when the driver is not in his seat.

'The driver places one foot on each pedal, and slowly presses down the left-hand one. The first effect is to admit gas under pressure to the pump, which is caused to revolve, and so start the engine. Further pressure on the pedal releases the brakes. Still further pressure begins to open the connection between the cylinders of sulphur dioxide and the turbine, and the car begins to move. Subsequent pressure continues this opening, until, when the pedal is fully depressed, the car is developing its maximum power.

'By this time the right-hand pedal has come out to its full extent. Pressure upon it will reverse the process. The gas will gradually be cut off from the turbine. Then the engine will be stopped and finally the brakes applied. In driving, the speed of the car is regulated by alternate pressure of the feet, using the left to accelerate, and the right to slow up.'

Oldland blinked, as his imagination grasped the idea. Ingenious, very. The Comet people, with their reputation at stake, wouldn't have taken up a thing like this if they hadn't been pretty sure of it. But, somehow, he didn't see that elderly chauffeur of his driving by alternate pressure of the feet. He would be lost without his clutch and his gears and all the other gadgets he was accustomed to.

Having thus satisfied his curiosity, and decided that the Lovell Transmission, in spite of its ingenuity, was not for him, Oldland would have liked to extricate himself from the throng which surrounded him. But that was manifestly impossible, until one of the periodical eruptions occurred.

And, at the moment, nobody else seemed disposed to move. The demonstrator had turned to a table, upon which were exhibited a number of metal objects of unusual shape.

'Here we have some of the parts of which the transmission is composed,' he continued. Oldland noticed now for the first time that similar pieces of metal were arranged at intervals all around the stand. The demonstrator picked up a piece of polished steel, the size and shape of a large mushroom. 'The speed of the engine is controlled by the amount of gas which is allowed to pass to the turbine. This, which is known as the pressure valve . . .'

He was interrupted by a commotion, somewhere behind Oldland's back. There was a sort of grunt, followed by a sudden cry, 'Look out!' Then a confused sound of voices. 'He's fainted . . . Nearly knocked me over . . . Steady there . . . Hold up his head . . .'

Oldland's professional instincts exerted themselves in a flash. 'I am a doctor!' he said loudly, struggling to turn round. A way was somehow made for him to the edge of the stand. There, lying on his back with his mouth wide open and a dozen anxious faces bending over him, was an elderly man, plainly dressed. He had grey hair, a distinctly florid complexion, and was rather more than inclined to stoutness.

'Stand back,' said Oldland. 'That is, if you can manage it.' And, by some miracle, the human mass obeyed him. Compressed to its utmost limit though it had appeared, it contrived to extend that compression a stage farther, until Oldland found room to drop on one knee beside the motionless form.

The salesman, thus interrupted in the full flood of his demonstration, merely shrugged his shoulders. A man had fainted! There was no novelty about that. He was the third, or was it the fourth, since the show had opened. It wasn't everybody who could stand a crowd like that assembled round Stand 1001. The salesman picked up the telephone which stood beside him, and rang up the first-aid post stationed in the building. 'Man fainted on Stand 1001,' he said languidly. 'Better send along the stretcher.'

Meanwhile Oldland had deftly loosened the unconscious man's collar. He put his hand over his heart and his face hardened. He straightened himself and faced the salesman. 'We must get him out of this, quick,' he said.

'All right, doctor,' replied the salesman. 'I've sent for the stretcher. It'll be along in a minute.'

Oldland dropped down once more by his patient, and began to massage the region of the heart. He was thus engaged when the stretcher-bearers arrived, having driven their way through the compact mass of humanity. The old man was lifted on to the stretcher, and borne away to the first-aid post, Oldland walking beside him.

As the stretcher was placed upon a table, Oldland resumed his ministrations. The first-aid post was well equipped. He called for a hypodermic syringe, and prepared a powerful injection, which he administered. Then he resumed his massage. While he was thus engaged a police sergeant drifted into the room, asked a few questions of the stretcher-bearers in a low voice, then stood watching the doctor.

After a few minutes, Oldland shook his head fiercely. As his hands dropped to his side, he looked up and met the sergeant's questioning glance. 'The man's dead,' he said curtly. 'His heart had stopped beating before I got to him. No chance of starting it again now, I'm afraid.'

The sergeant took out his notebook and pencil. 'What was the cause of death, sir?' he asked.

'Can't tell you that,' Oldland replied. 'The mode of dying was syncope, if that means anything to you. The coroner will order a post-mortem, I suppose.'

The sergeant endeavoured to write the word syncope, and failed after one or two attempts. 'I must ask you for your name and address, sir,' he said.

Oldland gave the required information. 'I should have thought that this poor chap's name and address were rather more important,' he added slowly.

'I'm coming to that, sir,' the sergeant replied. He approached the corpse, and very gingerly inserted his hand into the breast pocket of the coat. From this he extracted a bulging wallet, in which were a roll of notes and a few visiting cards. These were all similar, and were engraved 'Mr Nahum Pershore, Firlands, Weybridge.' The sergeant made a note of this, then pocketed the wallet. He glanced at the body irresolutely, then turned once more to Oldland. 'Is there anything more to be done, sir?' he asked.

'Not so far as I'm concerned,' Oldland replied. 'I can't bring back the dead to life. The rest's your job, I fancy.'

The sergeant still seemed dissatisfied. 'You couldn't give me a hint of what he died of, sir?' he asked.

'No, I can't. There are no visible signs of violence, if that's what you're getting at. The man just died. You'll probably find that he was suffering from fatty degeneration of the heart, or something. The best thing you can do is to get him along to the mortuary, and turn him over to the police surgeon.'

Oldland waited until the ambulance arrived, and then left the building. Both the crowd and the internal

12

intricacies of motor cars had temporarily lost interest for him. He went outside and regained his waiting car. Seeing his chauffeur's inquiring but very respectful glance, he shook his head. 'Not today,' he said. 'I'll come back another time, perhaps.'

He drove homewards, frowning over the sudden death of Mr Nahum Pershore. Professionally the incident was without significance for him. No doubt the post-mortem would reveal some morbid condition which would account for it. But it was an infernal nuisance, just the same. He would have to attend the inquest, and that would mean a loss of valuable time. Oh, well, it couldn't be helped!

His thoughts turned from Mr Pershore to the behaviour of the car. She certainly did run wonderfully smoothly. It would be a shame to get rid of her. If she were repainted and touched up here and there, she could be made to last another year at least. Yes, that was what he would do.

So the incident of Mr Pershore's death was not without its economic consequences. It reduced by one the ranks of the Potential Buyers. By two, possibly, since Mr Nahum Pershore might have intended to buy a car. But, upon the activities of the show itself, it had no effect whatever. Mr Pershore's body having been decently removed from Stand 1001, the salesman resumed his interrupted explanation. 'This, which is known as the pressure valve, is contained in a housing on the right side of the pump. Its function is . . .'

His voice droned on, inaudible, except to the intent group facing him, above the subdued roar with which the voices of the crowd filled the building. And up and down the alleys between the stands flowed the human stream, now pursuing a slow and steady course, now eddying about some exhibit of special interest. The incident of Mr Pershore's collapse had been witnessed by perhaps a couple of dozen people, none of whom knew that it had been fatal. So trivial a matter was scarcely a subject for comment. It may be that two acquaintances met by chance at one of the refreshment bars. 'Hallo, Jimmy, what's yours?' 'Mine's a double whisky and a splash. Seen that new contraption of the Comet people's yet?' 'Yes, I've just been having a look at it. Terrible crush on their stand. An old boy fainted just as I got there.' 'I don't wonder. Felt like fainting myself when I was there this morning. Well, here's luck!' And the subject of Mr Pershore would be forgotten.

That evening, soon after ten, when the last of the public had been shepherded from the hall, and the exhausted staffs were clearing up for the night, the sales manager of the Solent Motor Car Company was fussing about his stand. He was not in the best of tempers. Solent and Comet cars were in much the same class, and an intense rivalry had always existed between them.

As it happened, the Solent people had made very few alterations to their models for this particular year, with the result that there was nothing startlingly novel exhibited on their stand. Since novelty is what attracts a very large percentage of visitors to the show, this had resulted in comparatively few inquiries. And yet the Solent stand, number 1276, was very favourably placed to attract notice. It was close to the entrance, almost the first thing to catch the visitor's eyes as he entered the building.

The sales manager had a definite sense of grievance against his directors. If they hadn't been such a sleepy lot of fatheads, they would have seen to it that the works got out something new, and not left it to the Comet people to steal a march on them like this. How the devil could a fellow be expected to sell cars to people if he had nothing out-of-the-way to show them?

He happened to glance through the window of a resplendent Solent saloon, and something lying on the floor at the back caught his eye. He opened the door, and picked up a mushroom-shaped piece of steel. 'What the devil's this?' he exclaimed, frowning at the unfamiliar object.

One of his assistants, standing near by, answered him. 'It looks like one of the exhibits from the Comet stand,' he said.

'What? One of those people's ridiculous gadgets? How do you know that?'

The assistant, realising that he had given himself away, looked uncomfortable. 'Well, I just took a stroll round their stand in my lunch hour,' he replied sheepishly.

'Oh, you did, did you? And I suppose you've been recommending people who come here to look at our stuff to follow your example. And how did this damn thing get on our stand? Perhaps you brought it back with you as a souvenir?'

The assistant attempted the mild answer which turneth away wrath. 'I didn't do that. But I'll take it back to the Comet stand, if you like.'

'Take it back? Let them come and fetch it if they want to. I'd have you know that employees of our firm aren't paid to run errands for the Comet people. And see that you're here sharp at nine tomorrow morning. I want some alterations made on this stand before the show opens.' And, without vouchsafing a good-night, the sales manager departed.

His assistant watched him leave the hall. Then, since he

had a friend in the Comet firm, he picked up the pressure valve, for such it was, and carried it to stand 1001. There he encountered the demonstrator who had been holding forth when Mr Pershore collapsed. 'Hallo, George, this is a bit of your property, isn't it?' he said.

George Sulgrave recognised the pressure valve at once. 'Where did you get that from, Henry?' he asked suspiciously.

'My Great White Chief found it inside one of the cars on our stand. Somebody must have picked it up, and then, finding it a bit heavy to carry about, put it down in the most convenient place.'

Sulgrave glanced round the stand. There was certainly a gap in the row of gadgets which bordered it. 'Yes, that's right,' he said. 'Some of these blokes would pinch the cars from under our very noses, if they thought they could get away with them. Thanks very much, Harry. We shall have to have these things chained to the floor, or something like that. How's business on your stand?'

'Simply can't compete with the orders we're getting,' Harry lied readily. Loyalty to one's firm is a greater virtue than truthfulness to one's friend, as Sulgrave would have been the first to agree. 'We've sold all our output for next year already.'

'Same here,' replied Sulgrave, no more truthfully than Harry. 'You must come down and look us up when this confounded show is over. Irene will be glad to see you.'

'Thanks very much. I'd like to run down one evening. Good-night, George.'

'Good-night, Harry. Much obliged to you for your trouble.'

The attendants on the various stands completed their

labours and went home. An almost uncanny hush settled upon the vast and now dimly lighted expanse of Olympia. Wrapped in a similar hush, and an even dimmer light, the body of Mr Nahum Pershore lay on a slab in the mortuary, rigid and motionless.

CHAPTER II

Mr Nahum Pershore had purchased all that messuage and tenement known as Firlands, Weybridge, some five years before his death. He had got it cheap, since, as the agent who had sold him the place had observed, it wasn't everybody's house.

This was quite true. Firlands was an outstanding example of the worst type of Victorian domestic architecture. One felt that the designer's aim had been to achieve the maximum of pretentiousness without, and discomfort within. Still, nobody could deny that the house was ostentatious, and Mr Pershore liked ostentation. Besides, as Mr Pershore, who had amassed a considerable fortune by speculative building, could see at a glance, the house was solidly built and in excellent repair.

Mr Pershore was a bachelor, and he brought with him to Firlands his housekeeper, Mrs Markle. Long ago, fifty years at least, Nahum Pershore and Nancy Beard had played together in the builder's yard belonging to Nahum's father. They had grown up together, and perhaps, but for a series of events which had long ago lost their importance, they might have married. But, somehow, Nancy had drifted into matrimony with the son of Mr Markle, who kept the tobacconist's shop over the way.

Nahum had risen in the world, thanks to a certain pertinacity and acumen. Nancy had not. After twenty years of married life, during which she had encountered many vicissitudes, she found herself a childless widow with nothing but her wits to support her. For a time she eked out an existence by obliging one or two families in the neighbourhood. In fact, she had achieved the status of a charwoman. And then one day, casting about for something more lucrative and less exacting, she thought of her old companion Nahum Pershore. She sat down and wrote him a letter. It was indicative of the gulf which had opened between them that in this she addressed him as 'Dear Sir.'

Had she been inspired with some form of second sight, she could not have posted the letter at a more favourable moment. Mr Pershore was suffering from a profound weariness of housekeepers. They had come and gone, each more unsatisfactory than the last. Some had been young, and these had displayed tendencies which seriously alarmed the bachelor instincts of their employer. Others had been old, and these had been incompetent, and allowed the servants to do what they liked with them. He had just terminated the unpleasant business of giving notice to the last of them, when Mrs Markle's letter arrived.

Nancy Beard, or Nancy Markle, as she was now! He hadn't given her a thought for years. But he remembered her perfectly, both as a child, when they had been such good friends, and later, as a tall, lanky girl of nineteen. Tall she had been, certainly. Taller than he was himself. It may have been, though the thought did not occur to Mr Pershore, that that was why he had never married her. Or it might have been her ungainliness, or the lack of her pretensions to any sort of beauty. Mr Pershore, looking back, wondered what that thin-faced chap Markle could have seen in her.

Could he put Nancy Markle in the way of finding a job? That was the gist of her letter. Well, perhaps he might. She was within a year of his own age, neither too young nor too old. She had always been a dutiful daughter before her marriage, helping her mother in the house, instead of gadding about as so many of them did. It seemed quite likely that she would make him an excellent housekeeper. But . . .

It was this doubt that caused Mr Pershore to hesitate. He had only to shut his eyes to recall vivid pictures of himself and Nancy walking home from school together, or sitting with their arms round one another on a pile of timber in his father's yard. Had Nancy retained the same vivid recollections, and, if so, how would this affect their future relations? He looked at the letter once more, and the inscription 'Dear Sir' reassured him. He wrote to her, asking her to come and see him.

His misgivings evaporated at the interview which ensued. Whatever memories Nancy Markle may have had, she kept them strictly to herself. Her experiences and her present condition were in such striking contrast to those of her former playmate that, in her eyes, they now moved in wholly different spheres. From the moment of their meeting again, their relative positions were established. Mr Pershore was the master, Mrs Markle was willing and obedient servant. It was as though the very knowledge of one another's Christian names had been erased from their minds. Before the interview terminated, Mrs Markle had been definitely engaged as Mr Pershore's housekeeper.

That had been ten years earlier. Mrs Markle was now a tall, gaunt, loose-limbed woman with wisps of iron-grey hair. But she had turned out a perfect housekeeper. Mr Pershore very rarely so much as saw her. The smoothness of the running of his household, however, was ample proof of her efficiency behind the scenes. Mr Pershore allowed her a perfectly free hand in everything which concerned his domestic arrangements. Such matters as the engagement of servants were her province alone. Of these a staff of four was employed at Firlands. Cook, parlourmaid, housemaid and kitchenmaid. The garden was the care of a jobbing gardener, who came three times a week.

Under Mrs Markle's rule the domestic routine was regular, but not too exacting. Breakfast was served in the servants' hall at eight o'clock, and in the dining-room and housekeeper's room simultaneously at a quarter to nine. Lunch, if Mr Pershore happened to be at home during the day, or if visitors were staying in the house, was at a quarter past one. Mrs Markle, who was a very small eater, did not lunch. She preferred to make herself a cup of tea, with a slice or two of bread and butter, in the housekeeper's room, at any time she happened to fancy it. Dinner was served at eight, and supper, in the servants' hall and housekeeper's room, at nine.

On the day of his death Mr Pershore had left home, as was his custom three or four days a week, about ten o'clock. Mrs Markle spent the morning supervising the work of the household—she was by no means above taking a hand herself, if any of the servants had more than their

21

usual share of work—and telephoning orders to the tradesmen. There were no visitors staying in the house, and Mr Pershore had announced his intention of not being home until the evening. By one o'clock Mrs Markle had finished her morning's work, and was sitting in her own most comfortable room. She contemplated spending a nice quiet afternoon with her sewing.

But her peaceful occupation was rudely disturbed by the sound of running footsteps, and an imperious knocking at the door. Before she had time to say 'Come in!' the door burst open, and the cook projected herself into the room, and subsided into a chair, too breathless for speech.

Mrs Rugg had been cook at Firlands for the past three years. She was stout, and rather deaf, and Mrs Markle secretly suspected her of over-indulgence in gin on the occasions of her evenings out. But she was an excellent cook and thoroughly reliable. Never before had she been known to behave with such a lack of decorum.

For the moment Mrs Markle imagined that she had had recourse to some secret store of spirits. But, before she could make any remark, Mrs Rugg had recovered sufficient breath to gasp out her news. 'Oh, Mrs Markle! It's Jessie! She's come over terrible bad! In the kitchen. Gave me such a turn!'

Mrs Markle rose, with a swift movement characteristic of her. Leaving Mrs Rugg gasping in her chair she hurried along the passage towards the kitchen. Jessie Twyford was the parlourmaid, a pretty girl, the daughter of the postman, on whose recommendation she had been engaged. Mrs Markle, in spite of her haste, found time to wonder what could be the matter with Jessie. She had been all right, barely an hour before, when Mrs Markle had helped her to give the dining-room an extra turn out. Certainly Mrs Markle had noticed nothing amiss then. Besides, the Twyfords were a highly respectable family. Could it be?

She reached the kitchen, with these dark suspicions still unresolved. And, at first glance, she could see that Jessie was in a very bad way. She had collapsed into a chair, out of which she seemed to be in danger of slipping every moment. She had been very sick, and a hoarse moaning sound escaped from her parched throat.

A cursory inspection satisfied Mrs Markle that her suspicions were unfounded. 'Why, Jessie, whatever's the matter?' she asked, as she bent over the girl.

'Oh, Mrs Markle, I'm going to die!' Jessie replied despairingly, between her moans.

'A strong girl like you doesn't die as easily as all that,' said Mrs Markle cheerfully. She beckoned to the kitchen-maid, a strapping wench, who was standing by helplessly, with eyes wide open in horror. 'Take hold of her under the knees, Kate,' she continued. 'That's right. We'll carry her on to the sofa in the servants' hall.'

Jessie wailed piteously as they lifted her, but she seemed a little more comfortable when she had been deposited on the sofa. 'Now then, Kate, look sharp!' said Mrs Markle. 'Fill a couple of hot-water bottles, and put them on her stomach. Then see if she can drink a drop of water, while I go and telephone for Doctor Formby.'

She hurried away to the telephone. Doctor Formby, who lived a short distance away, and upon whose panel were all the members of the domestic staff at Firlands, was at lunch. On hearing Mrs Markle's account of Jessie's symptoms, he promised to come round at once.

Mrs Markle returned to her patient. Jessie was suffering

from a parching thirst, but every mouthful of water she managed to take caused a return of her sickness. She complained of cramp in the limbs, and continually tossed about to obtain relief. Mrs Markle was doing her best to make her comfortable when Doctor Formby arrived.

He felt the girl's pulse and looked at her tongue. Then he issued hurried instructions to Mrs Markle. Between them, they managed to wash out the remaining contents of the girl's stomach. Then Doctor Formby gave her an injection, and watched her until it had taken effect. He turned to Mrs Markle. 'She's been sick, you say?' he asked.

'Terrible sick, doctor,' the housekeeper replied. 'All over the kitchen floor.'

'Well, don't let them clear it up just yet. I shall want a specimen. Have you got any weed-killer in the house?'

'Weed-killer! No, there's none in the house. Bulstrode, that does the garden, may have some in the potting-shed. But I could easily send one of the girls into the town to buy some, if you're wanting it.'

'No, I don't want it,' replied Doctor Formby slowly. He wondered if it were safe to confide in Mrs Markle, and decided that it was. He knew her as a sensible woman, who could hold her tongue, and was not in the habit of becoming panic-stricken. 'I asked if you had any weed-killer in the house because I wondered whether Jessie could have taken any,' he continued. 'I don't want you to say anything to anybody else, Mrs Markle. But, between ourselves, this looks to me very like a case of acute arsenical poisoning.'

Mrs Markle gave him a horrified glance. 'Arsenic!' she exclaimed. 'There's never been anything like that in the house, to my knowledge.'

'I can't be certain, until I've had time to make a test,'

replied Doctor Formby. 'But it's only fair to warn you that I'm pretty sure of it. The point is, where did the stuff come from? She hasn't seemed depressed or anything lately, has she?'

'Jessie? Why, she's the most cheerful girl I've ever had to do with. Always laughing and singing about the place.'

'None of the other girls got a grudge against her, by any chance?'

Mrs Markle shook her head decidedly. 'Everybody who knows Jessie likes her,' she replied.

'Well, she must have taken it accidentally. Don't let any of the others have any dinner. It won't do them any harm to starve for a few hours. And try to find out what she's had to eat today. I shall stay with her for the present, till I see how things go.'

Mrs Markle went off to find the cook, whom she questioned closely. Jessie had had the same breakfast as the rest, none of whom had felt any ill effects. She had had a cup of tea at eleven, from a teapot which Mrs Rugg herself had shared with her. 'And apart from that, she's had nothing from *my* larder,' concluded the cook with conviction.

The housekeeper went up to Jessie's room and searched it diligently. She found nothing whatever to eat or drink, not even a biscuit or a packet of sweets. Then she returned to the servants' hall, and made her report to Doctor Formby.

'Well, it's very queer,' said the doctor. 'Stay with her for a minute or two, will you, Mrs Markle? I'll go and collect my specimen, and then the mess can be cleared up.'

He returned with a sealed jar, which he put in his bag. Then he resumed his vigil by the sofa, holding the unconscious girl's wrist. Not until half-past three did he pronounce his verdict. 'She'll pull through now, I think,' he said. 'She'd better not be moved for the present, but keep her as warm as you can. I'll send a nurse round, and come round myself in a few hours' time.' He paused, and looked fixedly at Mrs Markle. 'I'm going back home now to test this specimen. You realise that if the test confirms the presence of arsenic, I shall have to inform the police?'

Mrs Markle bowed her grey head silently. The idea of the police had been in her mind ever since the ominous word arsenic had first been mentioned. But, whatever would Mr Pershore say?

A rather awkward pause ensued, broken by a timid knocking on the door. 'Who's there?' Mrs Markle called out sharply.

'It's me, Kate, Mrs Markle. Sergeant Draper's here, and he's asking to see you.'

Doctor Formby and Mrs Markle exchanged startled glances. Sergeant Draper was a genial officer from the local police station. This was talking of the devil, with a vengeance. Had news of Jessie's attack and its cause got abroad already?'

'We'll see him together,' said the doctor, with sudden determination. 'I don't want this girl left alone. It had better be in here.'

Mrs Markle nodded. 'Bring the sergeant down here, will you, Kate?' she called.

Again that awkward pause, till the door opened and Sergeant Draper appeared. He was a massive, imposing-looking person, and usually wore an expression of the utmost cheerfulness. But now his countenance was one of portentous solemnity.

His eyebrows went up in astonishment as he recognised Doctor Formby and the unconscious girl on the sofa. 'I beg pardon for intruding, I'm sure,' he exclaimed. 'I didn't know that there was anybody taken bad in the house. Why, 'tis Jessie Twyford, surely!' He took a step forward towards the sofa, then hurriedly checked himself, but his eyes remained fixed upon Jessie's ashen face.

'You didn't know?' said Doctor Formby slowly. 'Then what brings you here, sergeant?'

Sergeant Draper averted his gaze from the girl, and fixed it on Mrs Markle. 'It's sorrowful news I bring,' he replied. 'Do you know where Mr Pershore went today, Mrs Markle?'

'No, I don't,' said the housekeeper. 'Mr Pershore doesn't consult me on his comings and goings. To his office, likely enough. He usually goes there on Monday mornings.'

'You didn't know that he'd gone to the Motor Show, then?'

'No, I didn't. But why shouldn't he, if he wanted to? It's more than once that he's spoken of buying a car.'

'Well, however it may be, he did go to Olympia. They've just rung up the station from there.'

'Rung up? What should they ring up for?' And then a sudden comprehension of the sergeant's meaning dawned upon Mrs Markle. 'There's—there's nothing happened to Mr Pershore, is there?' she whispered urgently.

The sergeant lowered his head. 'He's dead, ma'am,' he replied gently. 'Fainted away suddenly, and passed off without a bit of pain.'

Mrs Markle's face contracted, but apart from that she gave no sign. Her experiences before she became Mr Pershore's housekeeper had taught her to bear the hardest blows of Fate without complaint. The two men, watching her, had no indication of what was passing through her

27

mind. Memories of childhood, perhaps. Nahum's arm about her waist in that almost forgotten builder's yard. Or of the future, stretching interminably into lonely old age, pervaded with the smell of soap-suds and dishwater.

Doctor Formby was the first to make any move. He took Mrs Markle's arm and led her to a chair. Then he opened his bag, uncorked a bottle, and poured some of its contents into a glass. 'Drink this!' he said.

Mrs Markle obeyed him without protest. He watched her for a moment, then turned to the sergeant. 'Do you know the cause of Mr Pershore's death?' he asked quietly.

'No, sir, that I don't. All they said on the telephone was that a gentleman had had a fit at the show and died. They'd found a card in his pocket with Mr Pershore's name and address on it. When they described what the gentleman looked like I knew it must be Mr Pershore, and I told them so. Then they said I'd better come round here and break the news to his family. I thought the best thing I could do was to see Mrs Markle.'

Dr Formby seemed to give only half his attention to what the sergeant was saying. 'What have they done with the body?' he asked abruptly.

'It's been taken to the mortuary, sir. There'll be an inquest, and after that the relatives . . .'

'Oh, yes,' exclaimed Doctor Formby impatiently. 'I've never attended Mr Pershore, nor so far as I know has any other doctor in this town. But he's always struck me as a man of at least average health. Yet you say he has died suddenly from some unascertained cause. Two or three hours ago that girl on the sofa, who's at least as healthy as Mr Pershore, was taken suddenly ill. Queer, isn't it?'

'What you would call a remarkable coincidence, sir,' replied the sergeant. 'Is it anything serious that's the matter with Jessie Twyford?'

'That I'll tell you later,' said Doctor Formby. He went up to the housekeeper, who was sitting motionless in her chair. 'You'll be all right if we leave you, Mrs Markle? I'll have a nurse round here in less than an hour.'

His voice seemed to galvanise her into life. 'I shall be all right, doctor,' she replied. 'You can trust me to see that Jessie is properly looked after.'

The doctor and the policeman left the house. Mrs Markle, after seeing that her patient was properly wrapped up, went into the kitchen and asked Mrs Rugg to make her a cup of tea. Then she returned to the servants' hall, and drew up a chair to the sofa.

But her thoughts were not of Jessie, who now appeared to be sleeping peacefully. Her brain was wrestling with the sergeant's words, which refused to crystallise themselves into any credible fact. The idea of death and the idea of Mr Pershore were like drops of oil and vinegar, refusing to mingle. In her efforts to make herself realise that her employer was dead, everything else became of secondary importance. Even Jessie's illness, Doctor Formby's extraordinary suggestion that she had swallowed arsenic, seemed the merest trifles.

As she sipped the hot, strong tea, the central fact, though remaining incomprehensible, became fixed in her brain. Mr Pershore was dead. It was her obvious duty to inform his relatives without delay.

Nahum Pershore had been the youngest of three. Nancy Markle hardly remembered his two sisters. They had been much older than Nahum, had been out in the world when he was still a child playing in his father's yard. But she knew all about them. Rebecca, the eldest, had married young Bryant, who worked in the office of the local solicitor. A pushing young fellow, was Bryant. He had passed all his examinations, and become a solicitor himself. Then he had gone into partnership in London. The Bryants had an only child, Philip, who had adopted his father's profession, and was now a partner in the firm of Capes, Bryant and Capes, of Lincoln's Inn Fields. Rebecca Bryant and her husband had both died many years ago. But Philip was very much alive. It was only the day before that he had spent the afternoon and evening at Firlands.

Then there was Prudence, or as she was more generally known, Betty Rissington, Mr Pershore's niece. She was the daughter of his other sister, Naomi. Miss Betty must be told, of course. But, unfortunately, Mrs Markle did not know where to find her. She had been staying at Firlands for the past fortnight, and had only left that very morning. But where she had gone Mrs Markle didn't know. She was a very independent young lady, was Miss Betty. Liked going about on her own. But perhaps Mr Philip would know where to find her. Or Mr Philip's wife, though it was Mrs Markle's private opinion that the two ladies didn't take to one another much.

The housekeeper finished her tea, then, after calling in Mrs Rugg to keep an eye on Jessie, went upstairs to the telephone. She called up the office of Messrs Capes, Bryant and Capes, and asked to speak to Mr Philip Bryant upon a personal matter. She was put through and heard Philip's voice, 'Well, Mrs Markle, what is it?'

It seemed to her that there was a tinge of anticipation in his tone, almost as though he expected to hear bad news of his uncle. But she dismissed the idea, as having its sole origin in her fancy. Clearly and concisely she told Philip of Sergeant Draper's visit to Firlands, and of the news which he had brought.

So long a pause ensued after she had finished speaking, that she thought she had been cut off. But at last came Philip's voice again, high-pitched and irresolute. 'I can't understand it. My uncle died suddenly? And at the Motor Show? It's most extraordinary. I must have further details. I'll go round to Olympia now, at once. I think that will be best. Then I'll come down to Firlands as soon as I can.'

'Very well, Mr Philip. Excuse me, but do you know where I can find Miss Betty?'

'Betty? Isn't she staying with you? She was when I was there yesterday.'

'Yes, Mr Philip. But she left this morning. I thought you might know where she was.'

'I've no idea. It doesn't matter. We'll talk about that when I see you. Good-bye, Mrs Markle.' And he rang off.

Meanwhile Doctor Formby and Sergeant Draper had left the house together. 'You'd better come along to my surgery,' the doctor had said. 'I'll give you a lift in my car. Jump in. You'll find you've got another job in front of you this afternoon, unless I'm greatly mistaken.'

They drove to the surgery together, where the doctor told Draper to sit down and watch. He produced some chemical apparatus from a cupboard, and into it put some of the contents of the sealed jar, and then some fragments of zinc and acid. The mixture frothed and bubbled, evolving a gas which escaped through a narrow tube. Doctor Formby put his nose to the end of the tube and sniffed. 'Ah, I

31

thought so!' he exclaimed. 'Come here, Draper. Do you smell anything?'

The sergeant inhaled deeply. 'Yes, that I do, sir. Smells to me like garlic, same as them Eyetalian chaps do use.'

Doctor Formby nodded. 'Smells like it, but it isn't,' he said. 'It's arsenic.'

'Arsenic, sir,' exclaimed Draper, hurriedly withdrawing from the vicinity of the apparatus.

'Yes, arsenic. That's what we call Marsh's Test. And that smell of garlic that you noticed means that Jessie Twyford has been swallowing arsenic. Fortunately for her, she was very sick, or she would have been a dead woman by now.'

'Why, wherever did she get the stuff from, sir?'

'That nobody seems to know. Perhaps she'll be able to tell us when she's feeling a bit better. Now, look here, Draper, it seems to me that there's something devilish queer going on. Mr Pershore dies suddenly from some unexplained cause, and on the same afternoon his parlourmaid is found suffering from acute arsenical poisoning.'

A malignant look came into the sergeant's face. 'You don't think, do you, sir . . .' he began. But he seemed unable to finish the sentence.

'Think what?' the doctor asked.

'Why, that there was anything—anything between Mr Pershore and Jessie?'

'That's a question you can't possibly expect me to answer. If I were you, I'd get along to the police station and report the facts at once. You can say that I was called to Firlands by Mrs Markle, and found Jessie suffering from arsenical poisoning. That test you have just seen me do was rough, but conclusive. If further tests are required, I've plenty more material in this jar, which I'll seal up in your presence, I consider it most important that these facts should be made known to the coroner who conducts the inquest upon Mr Pershore.'

'Very good, sir,' replied Sergeant Draper. 'I'll see to it at once.'

CHAPTER III

It was due to Sergeant Draper's report, and to the action taken upon it by his superiors, that Philip Bryant found a stranger installed at Firlands upon his arrival there that evening. This stranger, a heavily built man with searching eyes, introduced himself as Superintendent Hanslet, of the Criminal Investigation Department.

Philip did not seem overjoyed at the presence of the intruder. 'I assume that your presence here has some connection with my uncle's death, superintendent?' he said stiffly.

'Hardly that, Mr Bryant,' Hanslet replied. 'I am here to investigate a case of poisoning which has occurred in this house.'

Mr Pershore's death seemed already to have had a disturbing effect upon his nephew's nerves. And the abruptness of this second catastrophe threw him completely off his balance. He took a step backwards, holding out his hands in front of him as though to ward off some unseen danger. 'Poison!' he exclaimed, in a queer shrill voice. 'What do you mean? Who's been poisoned, and by what? Has there been an escape of gas?'

'Shall we sit down, Mr Bryant?' replied Hanslet quietly. They were still in the hall, where the superintendent had met Philip upon his arrival. 'That's better. I thought perhaps you might have heard. The parlourmaid, Jessie Twyford, has been poisoned by arsenic, and I am endeavouring to trace the source of the poison.'

Philip's face became a study in profound bewilderment. 'By arsenic,' he exclaimed. 'What an extraordinary thing. And you don't know where she got it from?'

'Not yet. But I hope to find out very soon. Doctor Formby is here, and has gone to see whether the girl is in a fit state to be questioned. I expect him back any moment. Ah, here he is.'

Doctor Formby appeared, with Mrs Markle in attendance. He nodded to Philip, and then addressed Hanslet. 'We've got Jessie up to her own room, where she'll be more comfortable,' he said. 'She's conscious now, and there won't be any harm in asking her a few questions. But you'd better leave it to Mrs Markle to do the talking. It may upset her to be questioned by a stranger. Shall we go up?'

He made a gesture towards the staircase. Mrs Markle led the way; followed by Hanslet and Doctor Formby. Philip was left standing alone in the hall.

Jessie Twyford was lying in bed, looking rather flustered at being the centre of so much attention. The room was in semi-darkness, and as the three entered it, the two men stayed by the door, where they were invisible to Jessie. Mrs Markle advanced, and sat down on the edge of the bed. 'Well, Jessie, how are you feeling now?' she asked.

'I wouldn't be feeling too bad if it wasn't for my insides, Mrs Markle,' Jessie replied. 'And they do burn something terrible, just as if I'd swallowed the coals from the kitchen fire.'

'Well, you didn't do that, Jessie, but you certainly swallowed something that didn't agree with you. What did you have to eat this morning that the others didn't? Do you remember?'

A slight flush came over Jessie's pallid face, and her eyes filled with tears. 'It's a judgment on me, Mrs Markle, that's what it is,' she replied. 'But it'll be a lesson to me. I'll never touch anything that doesn't belong to me again.'

'Never mind, Jessie, nobody's going to scold you for that,' said Mrs Markle kindly. 'But you must tell me what it was you took. Just in case it should disagree with anyone else, you know.'

Jessie sobbed penitently. 'I'll never do it again, Mrs Markle. It was after you'd been helping me with the dining-room. I went into the study to look in the cupboard and see that there were enough olives in the bottle. And when I saw them I wondered what they tasted like, as I've often done before. And then the wicked thought came to me that if I took just one nobody would ever notice. So I opened the bottle, took one out with the fork, and ate it.'

'You shouldn't have done that, Jessie,' said Mrs Markle gravely. 'Did you only eat one?'

'No, Mrs Markle, I—I didn't. You see, it was such a funny taste, and I didn't know whether I liked it or not. So I took another, just to see. And then I thought I did, and I took two more. But that was all. I didn't have more than four, really I didn't.'

Philip Bryant didn't remain in the hall to await the return of the others. As soon as they had entered Jessie's room, he followed them softly upstairs. On reaching the landing he walked to the door of his uncle's bedroom and turned the handle. It was locked. So, he found, was the door of the dressing-room. He stood for a moment on the landing, overwhelmed by this discovery. Then he descended the stairs once more, and listened. Everything was quiet in the house. He picked up his hat and coat, and let himself out by the front door.

Mrs Markle, after telling Jessie that she mustn't worry over her theft of the olives, led the way out of the room. Without a word she went downstairs, followed by Hanslet and Doctor Formby. They walked across the hall till they came to the study. 'You have the key, superintendent,' said Mrs Markle.

Hanslet took from his pocket three keys, tied together with string, and tried them till he found the one that fitted. He opened the door and stood aside for Mrs Markle to enter. She switched on the light, and they found themselves in the room which Mr Pershore had called his study.

Not that Mr Pershore had been in the habit of studying. The room was really his own private fortress. When he retired into it, it was fully understood that he was busy, and was on no account to be disturbed. This rule applied not only to the domestic staff, but to visitors as well, who were tactfully informed that their host's business was of a nature that imperatively demanded solitude.

The truth was that Mr Pershore dearly loved half an hour's sleep after his extensive meals. The room contained a few pieces of heavy Victorian furniture, upon which lay a few newspapers and periodicals, most of which had not been opened. But the most conspicuous object was a huge leather-covered arm-chair, drawn up in front of the fireplace. Beside it was a small table, on which stood a tobacco jar, a box of cigars, and a heavy match-stand.

Hanslet closed the door and walked towards the fireplace. 'You did that very tactfully, Mrs Markle,' he said. 'I'm naturally very interested in these olives. Can you tell me anything about them?'

'I'll tell you what I can,' Mrs Markle replied. 'Some time ago, I think it was last year, Mr Pershore got it into his head that he was suffering from indigestion. Mr and Mrs Chantley were staying here for the weekend, and Mrs Chantley told him about Dobson's Dyspepsia Drops.'

'I know the stuff,' remarked Formby. 'Lots of my patients swear by it. Mainly, I fancy, because it has a particularly revolting taste. Some people judge the efficacy of a medicine entirely by its unpleasantness.'

'Mr Pershore believed in it,' Mrs Markle replied. 'He got a bottle at once, and has taken it ever since. A dose just before he went to bed. But he was always grumbling about the taste. Said he couldn't get it out of his mouth. And then one day Miss Betty brought him a bottle of stuffed olives, and told him to eat one after he'd taken the medicine. He found that took the taste away, and he told me always to see that there were some olives ready for him. They are kept with the medicine in this cupboard.'

She crossed the room to an oak corner cupboard, fixed to the wall. This she opened. On a shelf within it was a bottle, bearing a label, 'Dobson's Dyspepsia Drops. One teaspoonful to be taken as required,' a graduated medicine glass, a bottle of Crescent and Whitewater's stuffed olives, and a silver dessert fork.

'It was Jessie's business to look after this cupboard,' Mrs Markle continued. 'Mr Pershore used to pour out his medicine, drink it, and then take one of the olives from the bottle with the fork. Jessie used to come in in the morning, and take the glass and the fork to be washed. When she put them back in the cupboard, she used to look at the medicine and the olives. If either of them were getting low, she would tell me. The drops I got from the chemist, and the olives from the grocer. But I never waited until the bottles were actually empty. I always have one of each in my store-cupboard.'

'That's quite clear, Mrs Markle,' said Hanslet. He took the bottle of olives from the cupboard and examined it closely. It was about two-thirds full of olives immersed in liquid. The stones of the olives had been removed, and the cavity filled with a pink stuffing of pimento.

'Did this bottle come from your store-cupboard, Mrs Markle?' the superintendent asked.

'It must be the one I gave Jessie last Wednesday. She came to me that day, bringing an empty bottle, and asked me for a fresh one. I gave her one, and saw her take off the patent fastening and loosen the stopper. This must be the bottle.'

Hanslet thought for a moment. 'Have you any unopened bottles of olives in your store-cupboard now?' he asked.

'Oh, yes. I ordered one from the grocer as soon as I had given Jessie this one.'

'I wonder if you would mind fetching it? And I'd be very much obliged if you would bring a big deep saucer at the same time.'

Mrs Markle left the room, and Hanslet turned to Doctor Formby. 'These olives will have to be analysed, of course,' he said. 'If they are found to contain arsenic, Jessie's troubles are accounted for. But what I don't understand is this. She said she took four. But, by the look of it, more than four are missing. Mr Pershore must have eaten the rest. How is it that he did not feel any ill effects?'

'There's more than one possible explanation of that. They may not all have been poisoned, and Jessie may have been unlucky. Or they may all contain a small quantity of arsenic. In that case, one would expect the effects on Jessie and Mr Pershore to be different. Jessie ate four at once on an empty stomach, hence her symptoms. Mr Pershore ate one at a time, at intervals of twenty-four hours, after a big dinner. In his case, therefore, the effects would be more gradual.'

'Would they account for his collapsing suddenly at the Motor Show this afternoon?'

Doctor Formby shrugged his shoulders. 'I shouldn't have thought so,' he replied. 'I never heard of arsenical poisoning taking that form. But it will be easier to answer that question when we know the results of the post-mortem and of the analysis of these olives.'

Mrs Markle returned, bearing an unopened bottle of olives and a saucer. In outward appearance the bottle was exactly similar to the one in the cupboard. Hanslet took it, opened it, and with the help of the fork, poured the contents into the saucer. Then he counted the olives. There were twenty-four.

'The two bottles are the same size, so one may take it that there were appoximately the same number in the other,' he said. 'Now, we'll put these back again. That's right.'

Having returned the twenty-four olives to their bottle,

he marked the label with a large 'A' in pencil. Then he poured the contents of the bottle from the cupboard into the saucer, and again counted the olives. There were fifteen.

'Fifteen from twenty-four is nine,' he said. 'Allowing for the four eaten by Jessie, we have five to account for.'

'That's right,' Mrs Markle replied. 'Today is Monday, and Mr Pershore started this bottle on Wednesday last, five days ago.'

Hanslet nodded. 'It all seems to fit in,' he said. 'Thank you, Mrs Markle. We needn't trouble you any longer. The doctor and I will stay here and have a quiet chat. I wonder if you would mind asking Mr Bryant if he would be good enough to join us?'

Mrs Markle went out, closing the door behind her. 'I'm glad I thought of locking up this room as soon as I got here,' the superintendent continued. 'I took the precaution of locking up Mr Pershore's bedroom and dressing-room, too, till I had time to go through them. I thought I might find something fishy, as soon as I heard there was a case of poisoning in the house. And, from what I can see, somebody has deliberately attempted to murder Mr Pershore.'

As he spoke, he returned the suspected olives to their bottle, and marked this 'B.' 'I'll have both bottles analysed at once,' he continued. 'Now, if the olives from this cupboard are found to contain arsenic, how did the poison get into them? It's very unlikely that it did so before they left the grocer's. Mrs Markle opened the bottle and gave it to Jessie. Now, you know more about this household than I do, doctor. Can you think of any reason why either of them should want to poison their employer?'

Doctor Formby shook his head. 'Quite frankly, I can't,'

he replied. 'And, what's more, it would take a lot to persuade me that either of them had anything to do with it. You haven't lost sight of the fact that this bottle has been left open in an unlocked cupboard since Wednesday?'

'I haven't. The point is, who had access to it? The members of the household, in the first place. Then anyone who came to the house. But whoever poisoned the olives must have had a pretty intimate knowledge of Mr Pershore's habits. Do you happen to know anything about these Chantley people that Mrs Markle mentioned?'

'I believe I met them once when I was dining here. I remember her. She was a rather pretty, foreign looking woman. But I'm afraid I can't tell you much more than that.'

'Bryant will know all these people, I suppose. That's why I asked Mrs Markle to send him along. Ah, here he is, I think.'

But, when the door opened, it was only the housekeeper who appeared. 'I'm very sorry, superintendent, but I can't find Mr Bryant,' she said. 'His coat and hat aren't in the hall. I think he must have gone back to London.'

Hanslet frowned. 'I'd like to have seen him before he went,' he replied. 'Never mind. Come and sit down, Mrs Markle. I daresay you will be able to tell me what I want to know.'

Doctor Formby looked at his watch. 'Have you anything else you want to ask me, Mr Hanslet?' he asked.

'Not just now, thank you, doctor.'

'Very well, I'll just run up and have one more look at Jessie, and then I'll get home.'

Hanslet, left alone with Mrs Markle, adopted a disarming tone. 'You will understand that I want as much information about Mr Pershore as possible,' he said. 'And not only about him, but about his friends and relations as well. We'll begin with his relations. You have already told me about Mr Bryant and Miss Rissington. Are there any others?'

'No, for Mr Pershore's sisters are both dead, and so are their husbands. Oh, but I was forgetting. There was Micah Pershore, of course. But I don't think that he has been heard of for years.'

'The family seem to have indulged in Biblical names,' Hanslet remarked. 'Who was Micah Pershore?'

'Mr Pershore's half-brother. Mr Pershore's father was married twice. Micah was his son by his first wife, and Mr Pershore and his two sisters his family by his second wife. Micah was quite a boy when his father married again. He never got on very well with his stepmother, and he went abroad as soon as he was old enough. I don't think that he ever came home, and I never heard of him writing to any of the family after his father's death. I don't even know that he is still alive.'

'Well, now we come to Mr Pershore's friends. You mentioned some people of the name of Chantley, just now. Were they particular friends of his?'

Mrs Markle's eyes narrowed for an instant. 'Mr Pershore and Mr Chantley were very friendly at one time,' she replied. 'Mr and Mrs Chantley were often here for the weekend, but they haven't been down lately. Not since the beginning of the year.'

'Has there been a quarrel, or a disagreement of any kind?'

It seemed to Hanslet that Mrs Markle hesitated for an instant. 'Not that I am aware of,' she replied.

The superintendent did not press her. 'What visitors did you have in the house last week?' he asked.

'Let me see now. There was Miss Betty, of course. She was staying here all the week. But you can hardly count her as a visitor, since she is here as much as she is away. Then Mr Bryant came to lunch on Sunday, yesterday, that is, and stayed till after dinner. Mrs Bryant was to have come too, but she had a cold and stayed at home. The only other visitor we had last week was Mrs Sulgrave. She drove over on Friday and lunched with Miss Betty.'

'Who is Mrs Sulgrave?'

'She's the wife of Mr George Sulgrave, who is the son of old Mr Sulgrave, who was a great friend of Mr Pershore's. Mr and Mrs Sulgrave live in a house called High Elms, in Byfleet, quite close. They often drive over. Mr Sulgrave has something to do with the motor business, but I don't know exactly what it is.'

'Had Mr Pershore any other intimate friends?'

'Only Mr Odin Hardisen, who lives at Wells in Somersetshire. They used to see a lot of one another. Mr Hardisen used to come and stay here, and Mr Pershore would go and spend a few days with him at Wells. But I have an idea that they had fallen out about something.'

'What gives you that idea, Mrs Markle? Did Mr Pershore say anything to you about it?'

'No. It was Miss Betty who asked me if I knew anything. She likes Mr Hardisen, and she told me that she asked her uncle one day why he never came here now. He told her not to talk to him about the damned scoundrel Hardisen. Those were the very words Mr Pershore used, so Miss Betty told me.'

'And you've no idea why he called Mr Hardisen a damned scoundrel?'

'None at all. Mr Pershore has never so much as mentioned him to me.'

Hanslet made mental notes of all that Mrs Markle told him. Although they seemed to be straying a long way from the suspected olives, this information might come in useful later. And now he ventured to put a question which had been all the while at the back of his mind. 'It's rather a delicate subject, Mrs Markle,' he said, 'but do you know anything about the contents of Mr Pershore's will? Who he has left his money to, I mean?'

'Only what Miss Betty has told me. Mr Pershore never mentioned the matter to me himself.'

'And what did Miss Rissington tell you?'

'That her uncle had left her most of his money. Anything that might be over was to go to Mr Bryant.'

'Has Miss Rissington been informed of her uncle's death?'

'Not yet. You see, I don't know where she is, and Mr Bryant doesn't either. She left here this morning with Mr Pershore, and went up to London with him. She told me she wouldn't be back for a few days, but she didn't tell me where she was going.'

Having secured from Mrs Markle Bryant's address. Hanslet brought his conversation with her to an end. There was nothing more for him to do at Firlands for the present. He returned to London, taking the two bottles of olives with him. On his arrival at Scotland Yard he handed these over for analysis, asking for a report as soon as possible. Then he set to work to make notes of the information he had gathered.

Assuming the olives to have been poisoned, as everything seemed to indicate, there was no doubt that the attempt had been aimed against Mr Pershore. It could not have been foreseen that Jessie's curiosity would suddenly induce her to experiment upon them. But the attempt had apparently failed, since Doctor Formby was of the opinion that a sudden collapse, such as had been experienced by Mr Pershore, was not likely to have been caused by arsenical poisoning. On the other hand, it seemed probable that Mr Pershore had eaten five olives out of the same bottle.

The search for the poisoner was limited to the domestic staff at Firlands, and recent visitors to the house. Hanslet shared Doctor Formby's conviction that Mrs Markle was innocent. If Jessie had been the culprit, she would have hardly have gone to the length of eating so many herself, even in the attempt to avert suspicion.

It seemed far more likely that one of Mr Pershore's friends or relations was the guilty party. Hanslet proceeded to make a list of these, with appropriate comments. Philip Bryant, first. As Mr Pershore's nephew he was frequently a visitor to the house. His movements in it would be unquestioned. He had spent Sunday afternoon there. His behaviour had been curious. On being told of a case of poisoning, he had evinced an emotion which, while it might have been due to natural horror, might also have been due to a guilty conscience. And yet, on being told that the poisoning was due to arsenic, his emotion had changed to one of bewilderment. Finally, why had he left the house so unaccountably? His behaviour distinctly suggested that he knew more about his uncle's death than he had chosen to reveal. Yet, if Mrs Markle's information about Mr

Pershore's will was correct, it would seem that Bryant had very little to gain by his uncle's death.

Next came Miss Rissington. She had been staying at Firlands, and her opportunity for tampering with the olives had been even better than her cousin's. She appeared to be the principal beneficiary under her uncle's will. It was she who had originally suggested olives to him.

Micah Pershore, that shadowy half-brother, might be ruled out, at least for the present.

Then Mr Pershore's various friends and acquaintances. The Chantleys, to begin with. Hanslet felt pretty certain that Mrs Markle knew more about the relations between them and Mr Pershore than she had cared to say. But, since it appeared that they had neither been to the house for some considerable time, their opportunity was obscure. Even more obscure was any motive on their part for an attempt to murder Mr Pershore.

Odin Hardisen, the 'damned scoundrel' who lived at Wells. He had at one time been a friend of Mr Pershore's, but, quite obviously, they had quarrelled. But quarrels between old friends did not usually lead to attempted murder. Besides, in this case, opportunity appeared to be entirely lacking.

The Sulgraves. Mrs Sulgrave had been at Firlands as recently as the previous Friday. She might therefore have had an opportunity of tampering with the olives. George Sulgrave was connected with the motor business. This might account for Mr Pershore's visit to the Motor Show. He might have gone there on Sulgrave's suggestion, for instance. But here, again, any possible motive seemed entirely lacking.

The superintendent, having completed his notes, read

them through very carefully. As he folded them up and put them in his pocket, he shook his head. 'It looks to me as though that girl, Miss Rissington, had had a hand in this,' he muttered. 'I shall have to get on her tracks, I'm afraid. But, before I do that, I'll see what evidence crops up at the inquest.'

CHAPTER IV

Hanslet had not been long in his office next morning when he received a telephone call. He picked up the instrument. 'Who is it? Mr Merefield? Yes, I know him. Put him through.'

The connection was established, and he heard the well-known voice of Harold Merefield, Dr Priestley's secretary. 'Hallo, is that you, Mr Hanslet? Good-morning. I say, do you know anything about an inquest on a chap named Nahum Pershore, who died at the Motor Show yesterday?'

'As it happens, I know quite a lot about it,' Hanslet replied. 'Why?'

'I'll tell you. Oldland was here last night. It seems that he picked the fellow up, or something. He was telling Dr Priestley all about it. There doesn't seem to me to be anything very special in his yarn, but you know what my old man is. He jumped at it at once. And he wants to know when and where the inquest is to be held, and whether you can get him a seat at it.'

'You can tell him that I'll keep a seat for him, all right.

Two-thirty this afternoon, at the Kensington Coroner's Court. Is that all?'

'That's all. Thanks very much. I'll tell him. So long.'

Merefield rang off, and the superintendent leant back in his chair with a puzzled frown. What instinct had led Dr Priestley to evince any interest in the death of Mr Pershore? On the surface, there was nothing mysterious about it. An elderly man had collapsed in a crowd, that was all. Dr Priestley could know nothing about the curious incident of the olives. Yet that belligerent scientist, with his irritating passion for logical deduction, and his secret interest in criminology, seemed already to have detected an intriguing crime behind his friend Oldland's necessarily bald account of the episode.

Well, so much the better. Hanslet had already thought of paying a visit to the house in Westbourne Terrace and putting the facts before the professor. He had a way of sorting out facts which was very helpful. They would meet at the inquest, and Hanslet would ascertain the professor's impression later. Meanwhile he had plenty to do.

In the first place there was the analyst's report, which had just come in. 'Report on specimens submitted for analysis by Superintendent Hanslet, C.I.D. These consist of two bottles, marked "A" and "B" respectively, and bearing the label "Crescent and Whitewater's Stuffed Olives." Both bottles do in fact contain such olives, preserved in liquid. The bottle marked "A" contains twenty-four, the bottle marked "B" fifteen.

'The analysis was for the purpose of ascertaining whether arsenic was present in the olives, and if so, in what quantity. The method adopted was to test first the liquid contained in the bottles, then each individual olive, then the pinkish mixture used as stuffing.

'The first test was made upon the contents of bottle "A." In this case, the results were entirely negative. No perceptible trace of arsenic was found in the liquor, nor in any of the olives or their stuffing.

'The second test was made upon the contents of the bottle marked "B." On testing the liquor, it was found to contain arsenious oxide in solution. The flesh of each olive was then tested separately, and yielded positive results, though the amount of arsenious oxide present was inconsiderable. On testing the stuffings, however, each of these was found to be contaminated with a small but varying quantity of arsenious oxide. In some cases, the crystalline particles of the salt were visible with a low-powered microscope. The amount of the salt present in each stuffing varied, but the average was half a grain.

'This distribution of arsenious oxide suggests that the contamination had been deliberately carried out after the preparation and bottling of the olives. The method employed was probably as follows. The olives were removed from the bottle and treated separately. In each case the stuffing was removed, a quantity of arsenious oxide poured into the cavity, and the stuffing replaced. The presence of arsenious oxide in the flesh of the fruit could be accounted for by the absorption, and in the liquor by solution.

'It may be of interest to Superintendent Hanslet to know that the smallest recorded fatal dose of arsenic is two grains.

'The specimens are being retained in this department pending further instructions.'

So the olives had been poisoned, and Jessie's symptoms were accounted for. If she had eaten four olives, she had taken two grains of arsenic, and might consider herself lucky to be alive. But what about Mr Pershore? If he had eaten five, by the same calculation he had taken two and a half grains. And he was dead. This seemed so logical to Hanslet, that he felt sure the inquest would be a very simple matter. The medical evidence would reveal that the cause of death had been arsenical poisoning.

He made a point of lunching early, and arrived at the Coroner's Court in plenty of time. Dr Priestley was already waiting, and accepted the superintendent's offer to find him a seat with a curt word of thanks. Shortly afterwards other witnesses began to arrive. Doctor Oldland, who greeted Hanslet with a nod of recognition and a slight lifting of the eyebrows. The police surgeon who had conducted the post-mortem. And finally Philip Bryant, at the sight of whom Hanslet frowned ominously.

The Coroner reached the court punctually on time, and the proceedings began without delay. He was sitting with a jury of seven, and when these had been sworn, the witnesses were called.

The first was Philip Bryant, who described himself as a solicitor, and gave his address as 500 Lincoln's Inn Fields. He had seen the body of the deceased, and identified it as that of his uncle, Nahum Pershore. Mr Pershore was fifty-five, and lived at Firlands, Weybridge. He was a retired builder.

In reply to the coroner's questions, Philip stated that he had last seen his uncle on the previous Sunday evening. He had seemed in very good spirits, but not quite in his usual robust health. Asked what reason he had for saying this, Philip replied that he had noticed at dinner that his uncle did not eat as much as usual. 'I asked him tactfully after dinner if anything was the matter with him, and he told me that for the last couple of days he had been suffering from loss of appetite, with headaches and slight pains in the stomach.

'I suggested to him that he had better see his doctor, but he told me that it was nothing. He attributed his symptoms to indigestion, from which he had already suffered some time previously. I knew that he was in the habit of taking some patent medicine for this, the name of which escapes me. I asked him if he derived any benefit from it, and he told me that he did, and that he would take an extra dose that evening.'

'Did he appear in any way mentally depressed at his condition?'

'Not at all. He was as cheerful as I have ever known him, and spoke of going for a Mediterranean cruise in a few weeks' time.'

Philip stood down and the police surgeon was called. He gave his name as Cecil Button. He had been instructed to perform a post-mortem examination of the body of the deceased, and had done so that morning.

External examination had revealed no bruises or contusion of any kind. But, upon removing the clothing, a strip of linen, which appeared to have been torn from a shirt, was found tied round the right thigh. Upon removing the strip, it was found to be spotted with dried blood, not in any considerable quantity. Examination of the place from which the strip had been removed revealed three punctures, and on probing them, a corresponding number of pellets were found embedded in the flesh. These pellets had been removed. Doctor Button passed a small cardboard box up to the coroner for his inspection.

The Coroner opened the box and looked at its contents. 'These appear to be shot from a twelve-bore cartridge,' he remarked. 'Is it your opinion, Doctor Button, that these injuries contributed to the death of the deceased?'

'I hardly think that is possible,' the doctor replied. 'By the appearance of the very slight wounds, I formed the opinion that they had been sustained at least forty-eight hours before I examined the body, and possibly longer. They showed no signs whatever of being septic, and their position was such as to cause no danger, but only slight inconvenience. I noticed also that the skin in their vicinity was stained with iodine.'

'Did you form any opinion as to how these wounds had been inflicted?'

'They appeared to me to have been caused by a shotgun, fired at considerable range. The pellets were widely scattered, the punctures being rather more than two inches apart. And the penetration of the pellets into the tissues was not more than an inch.'

'You found no other sign of external injury?'

'None whatever, though I made an exhaustive search. I then proceeded to an internal examination. In general, the organs of the deceased were in a perfectly healthy condition, and showed the appearances to be expected in a man of his age. The heart, in particular, was perfectly normal. I formed the opinion that the deceased was a man addicted to good living, and that, at times, he ate and drank rather more than was good for him. But this indulgence had not resulted in any organic disease.

'Upon examining the contents of the stomach, and the

stomach and intestines themselves, I found slight but well-marked symptoms of inflammation. The nature of this inflammation suggested to me the presence of a small and not fatal dose of some irritant poison. I have made an approximate test, which indicated the presence of arsenic, probably in minute quantities. I have therefore sent certain portions of the intestines, and the contents of the stomach, to the Home Office for analysis.'

Hanslet glanced at Dr Priestley, to see what effect this sensational evidence would have upon him. But the professor's face was completely impassive. His eyes were closed, and to all appearances he was fast asleep.

The Coroner, however, was looking puzzled. 'Until we learn the result of the analysis, it is impossible to conjecture the amount of arsenic present,' he said. 'But you speak of minute quantities. Is it your opinion that the deceased died as the result of arsenical poisoning?'

'Not directly. For one thing, I believe it will be found that the amount of arsenic present was insufficient to cause death. And, for another, I have never heard of arsenical poisoning causing a sudden collapse without certain premonitory symptoms, such as vomiting. Further, with the exception of this slight inflammation of the stomach, all the characteristic symptoms of death from arsenical poison are absent.'

'Would you expect the swallowing of a small quantity of arsenic to produce the symptoms of loss of appetite, headache, and pain, mentioned by the previous witness?'

'Those symptoms are typical of chronic arsenical poisoning. I suspect the deceased of having habitually swallowed small quantities of arsenic, extending possibly over a period of several days.

'Upon continuing my examination, I found a character-istic appearance in the blood vessels and certain of the viscera, which led me to suspect that the deceased might have been exposed to the action of carbon monoxide. I therefore made a spectroscopic examination of the blood, and found that a small proportion of the haemoglobin had been converted into carboxy haemoglobin. This confirmed my suspicion that the deceased had recently inhaled carbon monoxide, as would have occurred had he been exposed to an escape of gas.'

'Were the changes sufficiently far advanced to account for the death of the deceased?'

'No, certainly not. The fatal effects of the inhalation of carbon monoxide depend upon the degree of saturation of the blood. The case becomes urgent when this degree of saturation reaches fifty per cent. But in the case of the deceased, I estimate that the degree of saturation was not more than five, or at the most ten per cent. Further, the cause of death in the case of poisoning by carbon monoxide is asphyxiation. In the case of deceased, the cause of death was certainly syncope.'

'Perhaps, doctor, you will explain to the jury what is meant by syncope?'

'Certainly. There are three modes of dying. Asphyxia, when the respiratory functions are arrested; syncope, when the circulation fails; and coma, when the brain is affected. The circulation may fail from the cessation of the heart's action, from loss of blood, or from localisation of the blood in one part of the system. In the case of the deceased, the last two causes are ruled out, and I am therefore of the opinion that death was caused by a sudden cessa-tion of the action of the heart. I can only repeat that I have been unable to find any reason for this having occurred.'

'Then you can tell the jury nothing more than that death was due to syncope?'

'That is all.'

'Do you consider that the other appearances you have mentioned were contributory causes of death?'

'It is very hard to say. They may have had a weakening effect upon the system. But neither by themselves nor collectively would they account for death.'

This concluded Dr Button's evidence. As he left the box, the foreman of the jury leant forward and spoke to the Coroner in a low tone. The Coroner nodded. 'Yes, certainly,' he replied. 'I will recall the witness. Mr Bryant!'

Philip reappeared, and took Doctor Button's place in the box. He looked ill at ease, and his fingers worked nervously as he clasped the wooden ledge in front of him.

'You told us, Mr Bryant, that you were at your uncle's home on Sunday last,' the Coroner continued. 'On that occasion, did he say anything to you about having been wounded recently?'

'He never mentioned anything of the kind. I noticed, however, that he had a very slight limp, as though his leg was stiff, but I put that down to a touch of rheumatism.'

'I see. Did you by any chance notice a smell of gas about the house?'

A sudden recollection came to Hanslet, of the brief conversation he had had with Bryant on the previous evening. On being told of a case of poisoning in the house, he had immediately asked if there had been an escape of gas. What had put that idea into his head?

His reply to the coroner seemed to answer Hanslet's

question. 'Well, now that you mention it, I did fancy that I smelt gas. I mentioned it to my cousin, Miss Rissington, but she said she couldn't smell anything. So I put it down to my imagination, and thought no more about it.'

'Can you account for the discovery of arsenic in the course of the post-mortem?'

'I cannot. I know of no source from which the arsenic could have come.'

'Thank you, Mr Bryant. I need trouble you no further. Doctor Oldland!'

Oldland entered the box, and described the collapse of Mr Pershore at Stand 1001. He detailed the steps which had been taken, and confirmed Doctor Button's opinion that death had been due to syncope. This concluded the evidence.

The Coroner, addressing the jury, said that he had no option but to adjourn the inquest. It would be necessary to await the report of the Home Office analysts as to the amount of arsenic found in the body. Inquiries would also have to be made as to the source of the poison. He would adjourn for a week, and he hoped that by that time additional evidence would be available upon which the jury could come to a decision upon the circumstances of the deceased's death.

The noise made by the rising of the court seemed to arouse Dr Priestley. He opened his eyes, looked about him, and got up from his seat. Then he walked up to the superintendent. 'It would afford me great pleasure if you could make it convenient to dine with me this evening, Mr Hanslet,' he said.

'That's very kind of you, Professor,' Hanslet replied. 'There's nothing I'd like better, but I've got a busy time ahead of me. May I look in afterwards, say about nine o'clock, instead?'

'Certainly, if that will be more convenient to you,' and Dr Priestley left the court, in company with Oldland.

Hanslet had been watching Philip's movements, and now intercepted him as he made for the door. 'I'm sorry you left Firlands yesterday evening before I had a chance to talk to you, Mr Bryant,' he said. 'There are one or two questions I want to ask you.'

'Oh, I was very much pressed for time yesterday evening,' Philip replied. 'But I could spare you a few minutes now, if you like.'

'Thank you. We can talk here. Nobody will disturb us now that the inquest is over. You, I understand, are a solicitor, Mr Bryant. Did you act in that capacity for your uncle?'

'Yes. He always came to me when he wanted legal advice, which was not often. He considered himself fully competent to manage his own affairs.'

'Are you aware of the provisions of his will?'

'I think I may say that I am. Some years ago my uncle consulted me about making his will, and told me his wishes. Since these involved my benefit to a small degree, I thought it best that some other solicitor should actually draw up the document. I therefore introduced him to a friend of mine, who took his instructions. I have never seen the will, but I am probably aware of its provisions.'

'Could you give me an outline of them? I am anxious to know who are the principal beneficiaries.'

'My cousin Betty—Miss Rissington, you know—inherits the greater part of my uncle's fortune. His wishes, as he expressed them to me, were these. He told me that his estate was worth between sixty and seventy thousand pounds. Out of this, he wished to leave Betty fifty thousand, free of estate duty.

'From the remainder of the estate, an annuity was to be purchased for Mrs Markle, his housekeeper, which would yield her not less than two hundred a year. There were various small legacies, to friends, and so forth. My uncle held a mortgage on a house known as High Elms, at Byfleet, of five thousand pounds. The house is owned by George Sulgrave, the son of an old friend of his. It was my uncle's wish that upon his death the mortgage should be cancelled, without repayment by Sulgrave of the sum advanced.'

Philip paused, and looked at the superintendent significantly. 'I was not aware until I heard the evidence of Doctor Oldland just now, that my uncle collapsed at the stand occupied by Comet Cars Ltd,' he said.

'Does that strike you as being in any way remarkable, Mr Bryant?'

'Not remarkable, perhaps, but natural. Let me explain. I should not have expected my uncle to visit the Motor Show at all. He was never interested in cars, in fact he definitely disliked them. My cousin Betty was always at him to buy a car, and, to humour her, he promised to think about it. But I am pretty certain that he had no real intention of actually buying one.

'Now, George Sulgrave is in the motor business. He has a job of some kind in the London showrooms of Comet Cars Ltd. His wife, Irene, is a great friend of Betty's. Whether there was a conspiracy between the three of them to persuade my uncle to buy a Comet car, I don't know. But Sulgrave may have asked him to come and look at the Comet stand. And, well, that's where his death took place.'

So Sulgrave was employed by the Comet firm. Hanslet resolved to add that fact to his notes. There might be something in the apparent coincidence, or there might not. 'I'm glad of that piece of information, Mr Bryant,' he said. 'But to return to your uncle's will. You said just now that you yourself were a beneficiary?'

Philip laughed, shortly and mirthlessly. 'Nominally, I am,' he replied. 'I forgot to tell you that Betty was to have the choice of anything she liked in the house, furniture and effects, I mean. My uncle would have left her the house itself, but he knew very well that she wouldn't live in it. I don't blame her, it's a beastly uncomfortable place. I'm what is known as the residuary legatee, that is to say that when all the legacies are paid, and estate duty handed over, I get what is left. I don't know, of course, what the estate will realise, but I very much doubt whether there will be enough to cover all the provisions of the will. In any case, the balance will be so small as to be practically negligible.'

'You have my sympathy, Mr Bryant. Was your uncle a man who had any personal enemies?'

'I don't think he had a real enemy in the world. He could be generous enough when the fit took him, and I think all his friends and acquaintances got on with him pretty well. But he had a way of taking offence over trifles, and that made him vindictive at times. I have recently had an instance of this.'

'Could you give me the particulars, Mr Bryant?'

'Oh, the whole affair is ridiculous. My uncle had a very old friend, by name Odin Hardisen, who is a wine merchant at Wells. They were much of an age, had known one another most of their lives, and got on very well together. About a year ago, Hardisen decided to extend his business, and my uncle lent him a thousand pounds for the purpose. And that started the trouble.

'There was no sort of agreement drawn up between them. My uncle wrote a cheque for a thousand pounds, and Hardisen gave him an I.O.U. in exchange. My uncle told me later that there was a verbal understanding that the sum would be repaid on demand, but Hardisen flatly denied it. He says that the agreement was that he should repay the loan at the end of five years.

'Some few months back my uncle wrote to Hardisen, I think more as a joke than anything else. He told him that he would buy his wines and spirits from him, if he would allow him a discount of fifteen per cent. Hardisen seems to have taken this seriously, and wrote back rather stiffly, saying that he could manage quite well without my uncle's custom, on the terms he suggested, but that if he cared to deal with him, he would allow him a discount of five per cent as a special favour.

'I think it was the tone of the letter rather than its contents that infuriated my uncle. Anyhow, he came up to see me, in a towering rage, and called Hardisen every name that he could think of. He showed me the I.O.U. and told me to write to Hardisen at once, demanding the immediate repayment of the thousand pounds. I tried to point out that this was hardly justifiable, but my uncle wouldn't listen. Finally, to pacify him, I promised to write the letter.

'I did not do so, thinking that in a day or two my uncle's resentment would evaporate. But it didn't. If anything, it grew more intense. Every time I saw him, he asked me if I had had any reply from that scoundrel Hardisen. I did my best to put him off, but it was no good. Finally, last Sunday, he told me that he had written himself to Hardisen, telling him that he had instituted proceedings for the recovery of the money. And he definitely instructed me to take the necessary steps, without wasting any more time.

'The whole thing is ridiculous, for if I could have persuaded them to meet and have a drink together, they would have buried the hatchet at once. But I fancy that Hardisen is just about as obstinate as my uncle. There have been other instances of my uncle having been seized with fits of vindictiveness, but he has always got over them.'

Hanslet nodded. 'This affair seems to have been a storm in a teacup,' he said. 'Just one more question, Mr Bryant, and I won't detain you any longer. When I was at Firlands yesterday, I heard some talk of a Mr and Mrs Chantley. I gathered that your uncle had been very friendly with them at one time, but had seen nothing of them lately. Is this another instance of a sudden dislike on his part?'

Philip smiled. 'Not that I'm aware of,' he replied. 'I've heard the Chantleys spoken of, but I scarcely know them, as it happens. Betty could probably tell you more about them than I can.'

'I am particularly anxious to get in touch with Miss Rissington,' said Hanslet. 'I understand that you do not know where she is?'

'I haven't the slightest idea. Betty has a heap of friends all over the place, and she's always dashing off to stay with one or other of them. But she's bound to see the notice of my uncle's death in the papers. I am arranging for it to appear tomorrow morning. And then she's certain to go back to Firlands.'

They parted at the door of the court, Philip to return to his office in Lincoln's Inn Fields, the superintendent to Scotland Yard.

CHAPTER V

Hanslet's visit to Scotland Yard was brief. After a short conversation with one of his subordinates, Inspector Jarrold, he caught a train to Weybridge, and very soon found himself once more at Firlands.

Mrs Markle welcomed him warmly. 'I'm very glad you've come down, superintendent,' she said. 'If you hadn't, I should have telephoned to Scotland Yard, and tried to find you there.'

'Why, has anything fresh happened?' Hanslet asked.

'I'll tell you. Jessie is much better today, and Doctor Formby says that he thinks she'll very soon get over the poison, and that it won't leave any after effects. I was up in her room talking to her just now. She's lonely there all by herself, poor girl. And while I was there, it struck me that Miss Betty might have said something to her about where she was going.'

'That was a good idea, Mrs Markle,' said Hanslet approvingly. 'Did Jessie know anything?'

'I asked her if Miss Betty had said anything to her, and

she told me she hadn't. But Jessie remembered hearing Miss Betty saying something to Mr Pershore about going to stay with her aunt. It was one day last week, when Jessie was waiting at table, but she can't remember which day it was. She heard Miss Betty say that on Monday, yesterday that would be, she was going to stay with her Aunt Chloe for a few days.'

'Do you know this lady's address?' Hanslet asked eagerly.

'Oh, yes. She is Miss Betty's father's sister, and she married a Mr Capel, who has a large farm near Colchester. Miss Betty often goes to stay with her. So as soon as Jessie told me that, I sent off a telegram to Miss Betty there. That would be about half an hour ago. I hope I did right, super-intendent?'

'You couldn't have done better, Mrs Markle. What did you say in your wire?'

'Well, I didn't want to give Miss Betty a sudden shock, so I just said "Please come back to Firlands at once urgent" and signed it with my own name. I thought I would break the news to her myself when she arrived.'

'Splendid! Miss Rissington ought to be able to get back here tonight. Now, I want to ask you a few questions, Mrs Markle. I've just come from the inquest on Mr Pershore. The doctor who examined him found that he had been shot in the leg, and that this must have happened within the last day or two. Do you know anything about it?'

'Shot in the leg!' exclaimed Mrs Markle incredulously. 'He never said anything to me about it. But, I wonder, now! I thought there was something very funny about it at the time.'

'Funny about what, Mrs Markle?'

'Well, Mr Pershore said that I wasn't to mention it. But, now that he's dead, there can't be any harm done. It was last Saturday evening, about nine o'clock. I looked out of my window and saw that it was bright moonlight, and that if there wasn't a frost then, there would be before morning. I didn't want any harm to come to the chrysanthemums in the greenhouse, so I went out to see that the windows were properly shut. Once, last winter, the frost got in and spoilt some of the best plants. Mr Pershore was very much upset about it.'

'I expect he was,' said Hanslet, as patiently as he could. 'You went out to the greenhouse?'

'Yes, and tried all the windows. They were shut, as it happened, and I was just coming back indoors, when I heard something that made me jump out of my skin. It was just as if somebody had let off a firework at the end of the garden.'

Hanslet considered this for a moment. Saturday had been the sixth of November, not the fifth. 'Did you find out what the noise was?' he asked.

'I went down the garden to see. I thought perhaps some boy or other had thrown a squib over the wall. You wouldn't believe the mischief those boys get up to sometimes. And as I was going down, I met Mr Pershore coming up. It gave me quite a turn, seeing him there in the moonlight. I didn't know that he wasn't settled down comfortably in his study after dinner.'

'Did you say anything to Mr Pershore about the noise you had heard?'

'I did, and he said it was all right, and that I wasn't to worry. He said that he'd found a wasps' nest at the bottom of the garden that morning, and that he'd just been down to blow it up with gunpowder, when the wasps were all inside.'

'Found a wasps' nest in November!' Hanslet exclaimed.

'Well, I thought it was rather late in the year to find a wasps' nest. But I didn't say anything about it. Mr Pershore wasn't one who liked to be questioned. And he didn't give me a chance. He told me that he'd had a tiring day, and was going straight to bed, and didn't want to be disturbed. I saw him go into the house, and then straight upstairs to his room.'

'Then he didn't have his dose of medicine and his olive on Saturday evening?'

'Not unless he came down afterwards and took them. Jessie would know if she found the medicine glass was clean on Sunday morning.'

'I wonder if you would mind asking her, and letting me know? It doesn't matter now. Any time before I go will do. What clothes was Mr Pershore wearing at the time?'

'His ordinary evening clothes, dinner jacket and black trousers. And he had put on an overcoat to go into the garden.'

'I'd like to see those clothes, Mrs Markle.'

'Well, it's queer you should say that. I can't think what Mr Pershore can have done with them. The coat and waistcoat are hanging up in his dressing-room. But I don't know what he can have done with the trousers. Jessie always put away his clothes for him, and on Sunday she came to me in a great state and told me that she couldn't find his evening trousers, or the pants he had been wearing. I told her to have a good look for them, and if she couldn't find them to put out another pair of pants and trousers. I meant to have a good look round myself on Monday, when Mr Pershore was out, but what with one thing and another, it clean went out of my mind.'

'We'll go up to Mr Pershore's room in a minute or two, and see if we can find the missing garments. Where was Miss Rissington when you heard that noise from the garden?'

'Miss Betty wasn't in on Saturday evening. She had gone to dinner with Mrs Sulgrave, at High Elms. She fetched her in her car, and brought her home again about twelve o'clock at night.'

'You didn't see Mr Pershore again that evening?'

'No, I don't think he left his room again. But not long after he had gone up, I dare say a quarter of an hour or so, there was a telephone call for him. But, as he had told me that he did not want to be disturbed, I didn't tell him of it till next morning.'

'Do you know what the call was about, Mrs Markle?'

'Yes, for I answered the telephone myself. It was a lady's voice, and she seemed in a great state of mind about something. She asked if she could speak to Mr Pershore, and I said that he had gone to bed, and that I didn't want to bring him down if I could help it. Then she asked if he was all right, and I told her he was quite all right, only tired, and that I'd spoken to him a few minutes before. And then she rang off before I could ask her who she was and if she'd like to leave a message.'

'What did Mr Pershore say when you told him about this next morning?'

'He didn't say much. Just thanked me, and said whoever it was they'd ring up again if they had anything important to say.'

'And did this person ring up again?'

'I can't say. There were one or two calls on Sunday morning, but Mr Pershore answered them himself.'

'You didn't recognise the voice, Mrs Markle?'

'I didn't. The lady seemed so excited I couldn't make out what she said hardly.'

'It wasn't by any chance Miss Rissington?'

'Oh, no! I should have known Miss Betty's voice. This was quite different.'

'Or Mrs Sulgrave, perhaps?'

'Well, I did wonder whether it could be Mrs Sulgrave. And then I thought that perhaps it was Mrs Bryant, Mr Philip's wife, you know.'

There seemed no point in pursuing this incident any further at the moment. Hanslet changed the subject. 'Have you by any chance had an escape of gas in the house lately, Mrs Markle?' he asked.

'There now! It's funny you should have asked that. Miss Betty came to me on Sunday evening after dinner and asked me if I had smelt gas anywhere. She said that Mr Philip had told her he thought he smelt something. But she hadn't noticed anything herself. I went all round the house at once, but I couldn't find anything wrong.'

'Well, shall we go up to Mr Pershore's room and have a look round?'

They went upstairs and Hanslet unlocked the door of Mr Pershore's bedroom. It was big and lofty, and packed with heavy ornate furniture. A smaller dressing-room, fitted with a bath, opened off it. Hanslet noticed that both rooms were fitted with gas fires, and that their windows were tightly shut. He sniffed vigorously, but could detect no trace of gas.

Mrs Markle followed his example. 'Seeing that these

rooms have been shut up all day without being aired, one ought to smell the gas if there's any been escaping,' she said. 'But I can't say that I notice anything.'

'Neither can I,' Hanslet replied. 'Did Mr Pershore sleep with his windows shut or open?'

'He always had them shut. He used to say that the night air was dangerous after one was in bed.'

'Well, now we're here, we may as well look for the missing trousers, Mrs Markle. You'll know best where Mr Pershore is likely to have put them.'

The housekeeper began a search of wardrobes and chests of drawers. Hanslet meanwhile took stock of the room. His attention was caught by an unusual object standing upon the night table beside the bed. It was a metal cup, standing upon three legs, and beneath it was a spirit lamp. 'What's this, Mrs Markle?' he asked.

Mrs Markle looked up from a pile of clothes which she was sorting. 'That?' she replied. 'Oh, that's what Mr Pershore used to use for his cough.'

'For his cough?' Hanslet repeated in a puzzled tone. 'How did he use it?'

'Well, you see, he used to be troubled with fits of coughing at night, which kept him awake. He tried every kind of lozenge, one after another, and they didn't seem to do him any good. And then Miss Betty brought him this home one day, and he was ever so much better when he'd used it.'

'But how did he use it?'

'He had a tin of powder, and he used to put a few spoonfuls in the cup. Then he would light the spirit lamp under it, and the powder gave off a sort of smoke which eased the cough wonderfully. The tin is in the cupboard under the washing-stand. I'll show it you.'

She opened the cupboard and produced the tin, which bore the label 'Hewart's Inhalant. For use with Hewart's Patent Vaporiser. Not to be taken.' Hanslet opened the tin and found it half full of a coarse reddish powder.

'That's it,' said Mrs Markle. 'The chemist gets it for me when the tin is finished. Now, what can Mr Pershore have done with those clothes of his? I've been through every drawer, and I can't see any signs of them anywhere.'

As she spoke, there was a knock on the door, and she went to open it. Hanslet heard her in conversation with somebody outside. 'Oh, it's you, Kate! A telegram for me? Is the boy waiting? Oh, on the telephone. I'll come down and take the message.'

She went downstairs, and Hanslet profited by her absence to abstract a little of the powder from the tin. This he wrapped up in paper and put in his pocket. Scarcely had he done so when Mrs Markle returned, looking very worried.

'No more bad news, I hope, Mrs Markle?' Hanslet asked sympathetically.

'I hope not,' she replied. 'The telegram was from Mrs Capel. I took it down as they spoke it to me. Perhaps you'd like to see it?'

Mrs Markle handed him the piece of paper she was holding, on which the message was written in a neat round hand. 'Betty not with us do not know where she is Capel.'

Hanslet frowned. He had not expected this. Then a bright idea occurred to him. Mrs Sulgrave! She and Miss Rissington seemed pretty thick. She would almost certainly know where this confounded elusive girl had got to. But would she say? It was worth trying. Better let Mrs Markle talk to her, though.

The housekeeper approved of the suggestion. 'There now!' she exclaimed. 'I might have thought of that for myself. I'll ring up Mrs Sulgrave now. She's sure to know.'

For the second time she went downstairs, and Hanslet, after locking up the bedroom and dressing-room, followed her. But Mrs Markle's telephone call was unavailing. Mrs Sulgrave was not at home. She had left on the previous morning, as the result of a telegram she had received from a friend of hers, who had met with a serious accident, somewhere in the north of England.

Hanslet bade a hasty farewell to Mrs Markle, and returned to London. By the time he reached Waterloo, it was after eight o'clock. He consumed a hurried meal in the refreshment room, then made his way to Dr Priestley's house in Westbourne Terrace, where he arrived just as nine o'clock was striking.

He was shown into the study, where he found the professor, Oldland and Merefield enjoying their coffee. Dr Priestley welcomed him with unwonted urbanity. 'Ah, you are punctual, superintendent,' he said. 'Sit down and make yourself comfortable. Oldland and I have been discussing the evidence which was given at the inquest on Mr Pershore this afternoon.'

'The medical evidence, you mean?' Hanslet replied. 'Did you make anything of it?'

'I think that Oldland, as a medical man, is better qualified to answer that question than I am,' said Dr Priestley.

Oldland finished his coffee and put the cup aside. 'I've just been telling Priestley,' he said. 'I know Button, who carried out the post-mortem, and I was so struck by what he told the coroner that I buttonholed him afterwards and had a chat with him.

'Naturally, he opened out to me rather more than he cared to in court, where he was on oath. He's completely fogged as to the cause of death. He can't really say more than I was able to say yesterday afternoon. Pershore's collapse was due to a sudden cessation of the heart's action. What caused that cessation, there is absolutely nothing to show. Button admits that it is the strangest case he has had to do with.'

'What about the arsenic he found in the body?' Hanslet asked.

'We can't say anything definite about that until we have the analyst's report. But Button has had a pretty extensive experience of arsenical poisoning. He told me that he was quite sure, from what he saw, that Pershore had not taken enough arsenic to kill him. Not more than a grain at the most. Further, he thinks that the arsenic must have been taken many hours before his death. And, as Button said at the inquest, arsenic doesn't cause a sudden collapse, without warning, and after a long interval.'

'Well, then, could the gas have produced that effect?'

Oldland shook his head. 'The carbon monoxide poisoning, again, was relatively slight,' he replied. 'Button is quite convinced that neither this nor the trifling wound in Pershore's leg could have caused his sudden death by syncope, and in that I thoroughly agree with him.'

'Then what the dickens did cause his death?' asked Hanslet incredulously.

'As a doctor, and relying upon the medical evidence alone, I should say that death was due to natural causes,' Oldland replied. 'There are cases on record in which the heart has stopped for no reason which medical science has been able to ascertain.'

Hanslet shook his head. 'That won't do,' he said. 'I know of one attempt, and I suspect another, on somebody's part to murder Mr Pershore. Would it surprise you to hear that I knew, as early as yesterday evening, that arsenic would be found in the body?'

Oldland laughed. 'Ah, now we're getting down to it!' he exclaimed. 'I'm quite sure that we shall be deeply interested to hear what you can tell us about that. Eh, Priestley?'

Dr Priestley's reply was to glance significantly towards his secretary. Merefield hastily provided himself with pencil and paper, and the three composed themselves to listen.

'I'll deal with the arsenic first,' said Hanslet. 'It's only by luck that that did not cause the death of a perfectly innocent victim. It's rather a queer story. I'll give you the facts, in the order in which I learnt them myself. Yesterday afternoon the Yard received a message from the Weybridge police, saying that there had been a case of arsenical poisoning at a house called Firlands, and asking us to undertake the investigation. I went down there, and this is what I found.'

He gave a detailed account of his visit to Firlands, and its results. Then he produced the report of the analysis of the olives, and gave it to Dr Priestley. 'That's what I meant when I said that I knew of one attempt to murder Mr Pershore,' he concluded.

'And what did you mean when you said that you suspected another?' Dr Priestley asked.

'I went down to Firlands again after the inquest, and made inquiries about the wound. Mrs Markle told me some very remarkable facts. These are they.' And Hanslet proceeded to recount his experiences during his second visit to Firlands.

75

'It certainly looks as if someone had a grudge against Mr Pershore,' said Oldland, when the superintendent had finished. 'What do you suppose really happened to him on Saturday night?'

'Somebody fired a shot-gun at him, that's pretty certain,' Hanslet replied. 'How and why I can't yet tell. The whole incident is utterly mysterious. What was Pershore doing in the garden at that hour on a frosty night? His yarn about a wasps' nest is merely absurd. And how did his assailant know that he would be there? He can't just have been lying in wait, on the odd chance that Pershore would take a moonlight stroll.

'But that isn't by any means the queerest thing about it. Pershore's own actions are what beats me. He gets those pellets in his leg, and what does he do? Raise an alarm? Send for the police? Not a bit of it. He spins Mrs Markle a yarn which even she finds hard to swallow, and goes quietly to bed. Not only that, but he takes every precaution to hide all trace of what has happened to him. The trousers and pants he was wearing can't be found. No doubt they were bloodstained, and he destroyed them to prevent awkward questions being asked. But why?'

'Perhaps because he recognised the person who fired at him,' Oldland replied. 'Being of a forgiving nature, he didn't want to get that person into trouble.'

'From what I can hear of him, his nature was anything but forgiving,' said Hanslet. 'He seems to have had a habit of quarrelling with his best friends over nothing. I'll give you an instance of that later. Now we come to another strange fact. About a quarter of an hour after the shot had been fired, an agitated female, who does not give her name, rings up and inquires after Pershore's health. She wants to know if he is "all right." Rather a curious phrase under the circumstances, I can't help thinking.'

'The whole affair is mysterious, as you say,' Oldland remarked. 'What's your opinion, Priestley?'

Dr Priestley, though he had attentively followed Hanslet's words, had as yet made no comment. But thus directly appealed to, he broke his silence. 'I do not think that we can assume that the shot was fired with the intention of killing Mr Pershore,' he said.

'Why, what was the idea then, professor?' Hanslet exclaimed. 'Do you think that Pershore was hit by accident, or that somebody fired at him as a token of their affection?'

'Let us consider the evidence,' Dr Priestley replied suavely. 'A careful study of the facts is always more profitable than conjecture. The spread of the pellets and the depth of their penetration suggest a shot fired at long range.'

'Ah, but wait a minute, professor,' Hanslet broke in. 'Don't you remember that curious affair at Riddinghithe, a year or so ago? Mightn't there be something similar in this case?'

'I will not deny the possibility, but there is no need to assume it. I will only say that, on the facts which are before us, the shot appears to have been fired at long range from a shot-gun. Now, I do not think that anyone would attempt murder at any considerable distance with a shot-gun, especially in the deceptive illumination of a moonlight night. The chances against success would be too great.'

'All the same, the attempt seems to have been made,' Hanslet persisted. 'The pellets were found in Pershore's leg. You can't get away from that.'

'I have no desire to evade the facts. But I feel myself at

liberty to place my own interpretation upon them. I believe the motive for the shot was to frighten Mr Pershore, or to deter him from committing some act which he contemplated.

'This theory, I think, will account for his subsequent actions. On Saturday evening he was performing, or was about to perform, some act which he did not wish revealed. He was seen by the person who fired the shot. He almost certainly knew or guessed the identity of that person. But, if he gave information against him, his own secret would inevitably come to light. His only alternative was to conceal the fact that he had been shot at, and this he appears to have done most effectively. But for his death two days later, the incident would never have been revealed.'

'Very well, professor, put it that way if you like,' said Hanslet tolerantly. 'It doesn't really make a lot of difference whether the shot was fired with the intention of killing or wounding. But you'll admit that the person who fired the shot also poisoned the olives?'

'I am by no means prepared to admit that without further evidence.'

'Oh, dash it all, there can't have been two people thirsting independently for Pershore's blood. Look at the question of motive. I questioned Bryant as to the provisions of his uncle's will, and this is what he told me. It's probably the truth, for he knows that I can ascertain the contents of the will, independently of him.'

The superintendent repeated his conversation with Bryant. 'Now, it seems to me that there are only two people who benefit to any appreciable extent by Pershore's death,' he continued. 'Miss Rissington, who gets the greater part of his fortune, and this chap Sulgrave, whose five-thousand-pound mortgage is cancelled. It may or may not be coincidence, but Miss Rissington and Mrs Sulgrave are apparently great friends. And both of them have disappeared without leaving an address.'

'Very thoughtless of them' Oldland muttered. 'Your idea being that they were in a conspiracy together to murder Pershore?'

Hanslet did not answer this directly. 'Sulgrave is employed by Comet Cars Ltd,' he said.

'And it was on their stand that Pershore died. Have you had a chat with Sulgrave yet?'

'Not yet. I've put Jarrold to keep an eye on him. I want to see if he makes any move of his own.'

'Did I understand you to say just now that Mr Pershore was of a quarrelsome disposition?' Dr Priestley asked.

The superintendent repeated Philip Bryant's account of the misunderstanding which had arisen between Pershore and Hardisen. 'There may be others besides Hardisen,' he said. 'But this isn't the work of an open enemy, but of somebody living in the house, or with constant access to it. The poisoning of the olives proves that. Besides, if it had been an enemy who fired at him, Pershore wouldn't have come tamely back into the house with his tail between his legs like that.'

'What immediate steps do you propose to take?' asked Dr Priestley?

'The first thing to do is to find Miss Rissington. She holds the key to the situation, I'm perfectly sure of that. I'm going to take the first train to Colchester in the morning, and interview this Mrs Capel. And if I can't get anything out of her, I shall have to tackle Sulgrave. I'll keep you informed of what happens, professor.'

As Hanslet left the house, he remembered the sample of Hewart's Inhalant, which was still in his pocket. He had become suspicious of everything he found at Firlands. Perhaps the inhalant had been tampered with, as well as the olives.

He therefore went back to Scotland Yard, where he left the sample for analysis.

CHAPTER VI

Next morning, Hanslet caught an early train to Colchester. It was the first chance he had had of thinking things over calmly, and he took full advantage of it.

The case was in many respects unusual. There was no direct evidence to prove that Mr Pershore had been murdered. As Oldland had pointed out, his death might have been due to natural causes. On the other hand, there was already very definite evidence that at least one attempt had been made to murder him. It would be an extraordinary coincidence if he had died a natural death.

The theory which gradually evolved itself in Hanslet's mind was this. Miss Rissington and the Sulgraves were aware of the contents of Mr Pershore's will. Since he appeared to have been a healthy and robust person, who might live for another twenty or thirty years, they had therefore decided upon his death.

Their first move had been the poisoning of the olives. Probably Sulgrave had prepared the poison. He had bought a bottle of olives, exactly similar to those favoured by

Pershore. Miss Rissington could have given him the necessary information on this point. Mrs Sulgrave had brought the poisoned bottle with her when she lunched at Firlands on Friday, and this had been substituted for the one given by Mrs Markle to Jessie on Wednesday.

The conspirators had probably no very extensive knowledge of poisons. They might have expected a single olive to be fatal. So that when Pershore turned up bright and smiling to breakfast on Saturday morning, they were more than a little flabbergasted. Miss Rissington communicated with the Sulgraves, and was asked to come over to dinner, so that a fresh plan could be concocted.

She knew that her uncle would be prowling about the garden at nine o'clock. Would it not be possible to take advantage of this? Sulgrave thought it would. He drove over to Firlands with a gun, lay in wait for Pershore, and fired at him. He did not wait to see the effects of his shot, but drove straight back to High Elms.

Here he found the two women impatiently awaiting his return. Mrs Sulgrave could not endure the suspense. She rang up and made inquiries. She asked if Mr Pershore was all right. Nobody would use that phrase unless they had a suspicion that he was not all right. She must have been dumbfounded when she learnt that he was apparently unharmed.

What happened next? A further consultation among the party at High Elms, of course. And the result of the conference was a decision that Sulgrave should try his hand again. He saw a means of murdering Pershore if he could entice him to the Comet stand at Olympia. There would be no great difficulty about that. Sulgrave would send him a ticket for the Motor Show, and ask him to come and see him on Stand 1001.

Pershore, with his avowed lack of interest in cars, might have refused. But Miss Rissington saw to it that he didn't. She kept on at him about buying a car. Even if he didn't want to get one at once, there could be no harm in his acceptance of Sulgrave's invitation. At last, for the sake of peace, he agreed to do this.

A very nice, closely-knit theory, Hanslet thought. He would do his best to verify it, point by point. It seemed to leave only one question unanswered. By what mysterious means had Sulgrave achieved his end?

The train reached Colchester. Hanslet took a taxi and drove to the address which Mrs Markle had given him. There he found Mrs Capel in a great state of excitement. She had seen the *Daily Telegraph* of that morning, in which appeared not only the notice of Mr Pershore's death, but a short account of the inquest.

'It's a terrible thing!' she exclaimed. 'I don't know what Betty will do when she hears of it. She was absolutely devoted to her uncle. I can't say that I was very much attached to Nahum Pershore myself. I always had a sort of feeling that he wasn't altogether to be trusted. And he had a violent temper, which made him say the most outrageous things. He was very rude to my husband once, and they've never spoken since.'

This was instructive, but it was not what Hanslet had come to inquire about. 'I am very anxious to get in touch with Miss Rissington,' he said. 'She was overheard to tell her uncle that she was coming to stay with you last Monday.'

'I'm afraid that must be true,' Mrs Capel replied. 'I had a letter from her on Monday, telling me that she was supposed to be coming here, but that I shouldn't see her till the end of the week.'

That letter must have been written after the conference at High Elms on Saturday night. This conformed with the superintendent's theory. 'You say that Miss Rissington was devoted to her uncle,' he said. 'Why then did she tell him that she was coming here on Monday, when she had no intention of doing so until some days later?'

'Well, you see, Nahum Pershore was apt to be difficult in some ways. If he took a dislike to people, he expected Betty to do the same. It was ridiculous, of course, but Betty had to humour him. You see, she has practically no money of her own, and depends upon the allowance he made her. And, besides, it has always been understood that she would come into his money.'

So Miss Rissington knew the provisions of the will. Another point in support of the theory.

'It would never have done for Betty to upset him,' Mrs Capel continued. 'I was always telling her that. And he'd have been furious if she had insisted on going to stay with people he didn't like. So we arranged a little deception between us, and I don't think that we can be blamed for it. Whenever Betty wanted to go to anybody that her uncle didn't approve of, she told him that she was coming to me. In spite of his rudeness to my husband, he couldn't very well object to her staying with her own aunt.'

'Under the circumstances, it is most unfortunate that this should have happened,' said Hanslet. 'Have you really no idea of Miss Rissington's actual whereabouts?'

Mrs Capel spread out her hands in a despairing gesture.

'Not the slightest,' she replied. 'Betty has heaps of friends, whom she has never told even me about. They're all perfectly respectable, of course. Betty isn't the sort of girl to take to people unless they are quite nice. In fact, I'm sure that all her friends are much nicer than her uncle was.'

'Have you any definite reason for disliking Mr Pershore, Mrs Capel?' Hanslet asked.

'Oh, I wouldn't say that I actually disliked him. Especially now that the poor man is dead. But I always thought—well, there now, he's gone, and I always hate gossip about the dead. It's only that I used to think sometimes that his morals were not all they might be. So very different from his dear sisters, especially Betty's mother. She was a saint on earth, if ever there was one.'

This feminine criticism of an elderly bachelor did not impress the superintendent. Mr Pershore might have fallen short of the standards of a saint on earth, but so far nothing disreputable had been alleged against him. Having satisfied himself that Mrs Capel was sincere in her declaration that she had no knowledge of the girl's whereabouts, Hanslet returned to London.

At Scotland Yard he found a report awaiting him. It was headed 'Report upon a sample of alleged inhalant, submitted by Superintendent Hanslet.' He read it and, as he did so, his face grew grave. Once more, and from another direction, the shadow of crime had fallen upon the ill-omened house at Weybridge.

'The sample consists of about an ounce of coarse, dark red powder. It is alleged to be a proprietary article known as Hewart's Inhalant. A tin of this article has been procured for comparison. In appearance, the genuine inhalant and the sample submitted are not dissimilar. But, while the former consists of a mixture of various harmless drugs, which give off medicinal vapours when heated, the sample submitted is of a definitely dangerous nature.

'It consists mainly of a mixture of powdered chalk and zinc filings, in approximately equal quantity, with the addition of a proportion of commercial Venetian red. The latter substance has presumably been added to simulate the colour of the genuine inhalant.

'The effect of heating this mixture would be the production of a considerable volume of carbon monoxide gas. This gas, by itself, is completely odourless, and its presence could not be detected by anybody breathing it. The sample contains a small proportion of the genuine inhalant, and, on heating it, the medicinal vapours would be given off simultaneously with the carbon monoxide. The substitution of the spurious inhalant for the genuine would probably, therefore, not be noticed by the user.'

So the presence of carbon monoxide in Mr Pershore's blood was accounted for! And one could hardly doubt that the same agency that had tampered with the olives had substituted the spurious inhalant for the genuine article.

Hanslet realised that this conformed to the theory he had formed. The conspirators had not put their trust in the olives alone. They had employed a second method of poisoning as well. They had meant to make quite sure of their victim. It was remarkable, when one came to think of it, that they had been so impatient. Both arsenic and carbon monoxide were cumulative poisons, as Hanslet knew. If Mr Pershore had been allowed to continue to eat his olives, and breathe his inhalant, either or both would have killed him in time. But perhaps they had not known that. Or perhaps they were afraid that Mr Pershore's suspicions would be aroused. He might have noticed a peculiar flavour in the olives, or some slight difference in the behaviour of the inhalant when heated.

But the superintendent had no time to waste in surmise. He was anxious to explore Firlands by daylight, and if he was to do so that day he must get a move on. He left Scotland Yard and, for the third time, made the journey to Weybridge.

Mrs Markle was growing accustomed to his visits, and welcomed him without surprise. 'Jessie's ever so much better,' she said. 'Doctor Formby is very pleased with her. Oh, and I asked her yesterday evening, after you had gone, if she remembered washing Mr Pershore's medicine glass on Sunday. She told me that when she went into the study that morning to fetch it, she found that it was clean, and had not been used. The fork which was kept in the cupboard for Mr Pershore to get the olives out of the bottle with hadn't been used either.'

'Thank you, Mrs Markle. I'm glad to know that,' Hanslet replied. 'Now, I wonder if you would mind taking me into the garden, and showing me where you were standing when you heard that noise on Saturday evening?'

'I'll do that with pleasure,' said the housekeeper. 'The quickest way will be for us to go out by the side door.'

She led the way across the hall and opened a baize door at the farther side of it. This door Hanslet noticed for the first time, since it had been open and hooked back against the wall on the occasion of his previous visits to the house. He now saw that when not hooked back it was kept closed by a spring. Beyond this door was a short passage, off which opened on the left Mr Pershore's study, and on the right a cloak-room and lavatory. The passage terminated in another door, with ground glass panels. Mrs Markle opened this and, on descending a couple of steps, they found themselves in the garden.

'One moment, Mrs Markle,' said Hanslet. 'When you went out on Saturday evening to look at the greenhouse windows, did you leave the house by this door?'

'Oh, no, I should never have thought of doing that,' she replied. 'Mr Pershore didn't like anybody using this passage but himself. He always looked upon this as his own private part of the house, where he need not be disturbed. That is why he had the baize door put up at the end of the passage, so that he could be cut off from the rest of the house. On Saturday evening I went out by the front door, and walked round the outside.'

'Mr Pershore had no objection to Miss Rissington using this door if she wanted to, I suppose?' Hanslet remarked.

'He didn't like anybody to use it, even Miss Betty. If she wanted to go out into the garden, she always used the front door.'

Hanslet stood at the foot of the steps and looked out over the garden, dark and dreary in the gloom of the November afternoon. It was more extensive than he had anticipated, being perhaps two or three acres in all. A high wooden paling ran all round it, and inside this was a row of tall trees, with shrubs between them. Whoever had laid out the garden had taken every precaution that it should not be overlooked.

This enclosed space had a melancholy appearance. No doubt in summer it was a delightfully shady retreat. Now it was about as cheerful as a graveyard. It consisted mainly of rough grass, in which were set a few beds, now bare of flowers, and here and there a straggling and untended group of shrubs. The gravelled paths were overgrown and unweeded, and upon these the overshadowing trees dripped relentlessly.

Mrs Markle must have guessed what was passing through the superintendent's mind. 'It's not very tidy, I'm afraid,' she said apologetically. 'But then, you see, Mr Pershore never took an interest in the garden. Bulstrode does his best, I'm sure, but he only comes three times a week, and there's more ground than he can manage properly. It looks better in summer, for Miss Betty always sees that the beds are filled with geraniums, or something bright like that.'

'It could do with a bit of brightening up,' Hanslet replied. 'Now, where's this greenhouse, Mrs Markle?'

'Just round the corner of the house.' They walked along the path, under the study window, and reached a small lean-to structure, which badly needed a coat of paint. Within it were a few plants which the superintendent recognised as chrysanthemums. Outside the door of the greenhouse, Mrs Markle stopped. 'This is where I was standing when I heard that noise,' she said. 'It seemed to come from the bottom of the garden.'

'I see. And you started to walk in that direction. Will you show me?'

She set off down the path, Hanslet following her. The lower part of the garden was hidden from them by an intervening shrubbery round which the path wound its way. Just as they reached this shrubbery, Mrs Markle stopped a second time. 'This is where I met Mr Pershore, and spoke to him,' she said.

'After he had told you about the wasps' nest he went into the house, didn't he? Which door did he go in by?'

'The side door, the one we came out of just now. I went round to the front door, and by the time I got in he was at the top of the stairs. I heard him go into his bedroom and shut the door.'

'I'd rather like to go down to the bottom of the garden and see if there are any signs of that wasps' nest,' said Hanslet.

The path circled round the shrubbery, revealing a waste of kitchen garden, untended like the rest. The greater part was occupied by plants of the cabbage tribe, exhaling a rank smell in the damp atmosphere. Elsewhere it was weed-grown, save for one patch which had been recently dug over. This was the only sign of Bulstrode's activities.

'You thought the noise came from somewhere down here?' asked Hanslet?

'That's what it sounded like. But of course it's very difficult to tell where a sound does come from, especially at night. And it's a funny thing that Mr Pershore should have thought of blowing up a nest with gunpowder. I never heard of anybody doing that.'

'Are you much troubled with wasps here?'

'Sometimes we get a lot, especially about the time the fruit is ripe. Bulstrode finds a nest occasionally. But then he comes up to the house and gets some paraffin and pours it in. I never heard of Mr Pershore finding one before. He must have noticed it one day when he was walking through the garden.'

'Did he often walk through the garden? I thought you told me that it didn't interest him?'

'Oh, no, it didn't. But then, you see, he often walked down this way to get to the gate at the bottom. I'll show you where that is, if you like.'

She led the way to the extreme end of the kitchen garden. There, set in the surrounding paling, was a narrow door. The superintendent tried the handle, and found it locked.

'It's always kept locked,' Mrs Markle explained. 'Mr Pershore had the key, and used to carry it in his pocket. Nobody else ever used this door but him.'

'What's on the other side of it?' Hanslet asked.

'A narrow lane, which runs between this house and the next. It's all rough and muddy. I should never think of using it, myself. But Mr Pershore always said that it was the shortest way to walk to the station. It may save a few yards, but I'd far rather go round by the road. The lane's so dirty, and very dark at night.'

Hanslet nodded. But he was only giving half his attention to what Mrs Markle was saying. He was thinking of Dr Priestley's remark of the previous evening. Mr Pershore, when he was shot, might have been engaged upon some business the nature of which he wished to remain secret.

There might be something in this, after all. Pershore seemed to have arranged matters so that he could enter or leave the house without anyone being a penny the wiser. That prohibition against anyone but himself using the passage by the study. The provision of the baize door, as a barrier against observation. The side door, sacred to himself. And now this entry from the lane, of which he alone possessed the key. Everything suggested that he might have had affairs which he guarded in jealous secrecy from the rest of the household.

And even from his niece. But, had she by any chance learnt the secret? Was there some hitherto unguessed motive for murder, unconnected with the provisions of Pershore's will? And, if Miss Rissington knew the secret, who shared this knowledge with her? Her cousin, Philip Bryant? Her intimate friends, the Sulgraves? There was something about the mysterious and dismal hush of this neglected garden that drove the superintendent's thought into channels of morbid speculation.

As he turned away from the locked door, he caught sight of a cylindrical object, standing in the centre of the patch of waste ground. It was made of galvanised iron, and was surmounted by a low chimney, of the same material. 'What's that, Mrs Markle?' he asked as he pointed to it.

'That's what Mr Pershore bought to burn up the rubbish in,' she replied. 'Bulstrode calls it an insinuator, but I don't know whether that's the proper name or not.'

'Insinuator? Oh, I expect he means incinerator. What sort of rubbish is burnt in it?'

'All the rubbish from the house. It's put in the refuse bin, and Bulstrode brings it down here when he comes and burns it.'

Hanslet was struck with an idea. He walked across to the incinerator and lifted the lid. Inside was a small heap of damp ashes. Evidently nothing had been burnt in it for the last couple of days.

Nearby was a pile of half rotted pea-sticks. With one of these he raked out the ashes and ran his fingers through them. He was rewarded by the discovery of a dozen or so trouser buttons, all showing signs of having been subjected to the action of fire.

Mrs Markle watched these strange proceedings with unconcealed surprise. 'Why, whatever have you got there, superintendent?' she asked.

Hanslet held them out for inspection. 'What do you think they are, Mrs Markle?'

'Why, they're trouser buttons! However did they come to be there? I'm sure that none of the girls would ever throw away good buttons with the rubbish.'

'No, they wouldn't be likely to do that. I think the buttons were put in here while they were still sewn to the trousers to which they belonged. In fact, I'm pretty sure that they are all you will ever see of Mr Pershore's best evening trousers.'

'Well, I never!' Mrs Markle exclaimed. 'I've hunted high and low for those trousers, and I can't find them anywhere. But whoever would have burnt a good pair like that?'

'Perhaps Mr Pershore burnt them himself, having no further use for them.'

Mrs Markle shook her head vigorously. 'He'd never do that,' she replied with conviction. 'He always used to let me have his old clothes to give away to anybody who wanted them. And those trousers weren't old. Why, he only had them at the beginning of the year.'

Hanslet did not think fit to enlighten Mrs Markle as to her employer's possible motives for destroying his trousers. They walked back to the house together, and shortly afterwards Hanslet took his leave. He returned to Scotland Yard, and, on reaching his office, found Jarrold waiting for him. 'Well, what's your news?' he asked.

'I've made the inquiries you told me to,' Jarrold replied. 'We'll take Pershore first, shall we? He seems to have been a harmless enough old boy, from what I can hear. He made a very good thing out of speculative building in the suburbs, and retired a few years ago, just before he bought that house at Weybridge.'

'Well, if he had retired, what about that office that he's supposed to have been in the habit of going to?'

'That's all right. This is the way of it. When he retired, he liked the idea of still having a finger in the pie. So he retained an interest in a firm of builders with an office in Lambeth. He was on the board of directors, and used to blow into the office three or four times a week.

'I had a chat with the manager, who seems to have liked Pershore well enough. He admitted that he was a bit testy at times, but otherwise, taking him all round, he was a very decent fellow. His attendance at the office was only to give him something to do. He'd turn up, have a yarn, and then go off to lunch. The last time he was there was on Friday morning.'

'He didn't put in an appearance on Monday, then?' Hanslet asked.

'No. He told the people in the office on Friday that they wouldn't see him again till Tuesday.'

'Right. Now what about Sulgrave?'

'Sulgrave is in the London showrooms of the Comet Cars Ltd. Somewhere round about thirty, married, and lives at High Elms, Byfleet. Is generally supposed to have money beyond his salary. Sort of chap who believes in a high standard of living. Popular with his friends, and no notorious vices.

'I hadn't much difficulty in establishing his movements during the last few days. The Motor Show opened on Thursday the fourth. On the night of Wednesday the third he took a room at an hotel in Kensington. He has slept there every night since. During the daytime he is on the Comet stand at Olympia from before ten in the morning until after ten at night. The Motor Show not being open on Sunday, he went home in the morning, but he was back at his hotel before midnight.'

Hanslet frowned. This dealt a blow to his carefully elaborated theory. 'Are you sure that he was on the stand at Olympia at nine o'clock on Saturday evening?' he asked.

'Certain. He didn't leave it until about half-past ten, and then went straight back to his hotel. There's not the slightest doubt about that.'

'He was on the stand all day Monday?'

'On and off. He never left Olympia. He went to lunch in the dining-room at half-past twelve, and was back on the stand by half-past one. He was actually demonstrating this new transmission that the Comet people have got out when Pershore collapsed.'

'What did he do when that happened?'

'Just went on demonstrating. I've been to the stand, and had a look at things for myself, though I was careful to say nothing to Sulgrave. There's a mob of people round it all day. They crowd on to the stand until there's hardly room to move. There wouldn't be the slightest chance of anybody on the stand recognising an individual at the back of the crowd. Sulgrave wouldn't have seen Pershore, and he wouldn't know who it was that had fainted. They're quite used to that sort of thing, I'm told.'

'Have you found out anything about Mrs Sulgrave?'

'Nothing fresh. She had a telephone message on Monday morning, and rushed off at once to look after a friend who had been hurt in an accident in the north of England. Or so she told her maid. Nothing has been heard of her since.'

'All right. Keep an eye on High Elms, and if Mrs Sulgrave turns up, let me know.'

Jarrold went out, and Hanslet turned to the pile of documents awaiting his attention. He was thus engaged when a messenger brought him an envelope. Within it was a copy of the report of the Home Office pathologist upon the material sent him by Doctor Button.

The main body of the report was couched in technical terms beyond the superintendent's comprehension. But there was a note at the end, summarising the results in plain langugage.

'It will be seen that the evidence shows that arsenic, in the form of arsenious oxide, had entered the system of the deceased by way of the mouth. But this evidence does not point to arsenical poisoning as the cause of death. The amount of arsenic present was very small, and suggests that the poison was taken in non-fatal doses, spread over a period of three or four days.

'Arsenic is a cumulative poison, and these small doses, if continued, would probably have resulted in a condition of chronic arsenical poison, and eventual death. But, at the time of the death of the deceased, the total amount of arsenic was probably no more than a grain at most.

'The fact that only traces of arsenic were found in the contents of the stomach suggest that the last dose was taken many hours before death. The deceased had had a meal shortly before he died, but it can be stated with certainty that no substance containing arsenic was consumed in the course of this meal.'

Hanslet put the report in his pocket and returned to a perusal of the documents.

CHAPTER VII

'I promised to keep you in touch with this Pershore business, professor,' said Hanslet. 'I've been busy on it all day, and I've learnt a few things which it may interest you to hear.'

He was sitting in Dr Priestley's study on Wednesday evening. Dr Oldland was not present, but Dr Priestley and Merefield formed an attentive audience.

'I shall be very glad to hear anything you may care to tell me,' Dr Priestley replied.

Hanslet gave a detailed account of his proceedings during the day. 'Now, let's see what we can piece together,' he continued. 'I got nothing from my journey to Colchester. Mrs Capel was speaking the truth, I'm quite sure of that. She doesn't know where Miss Rissington is, and she can't offer any suggestion. And it's a very odd thing that, although the notice of Pershore's death appeared in the papers this morning, Miss Rissington has made no sign. I rang up Mrs Markle just before I came here, and she's heard nothing from her.'

'I should not say that your time spent in interviewing Mrs Capel was entirely wasted,' Dr Priestley replied. 'You at least obtained her views upon Mr Pershore's character, and on the relationship between him and his niece.'

'Yes, but I don't see what good that is. Mrs Capel doesn't consider that Pershore's morals were above reproach. Well, I dare say they weren't, though nobody else seems to have noticed the fact. It can't have had any bearing on his death, that's quite certain.'

'Why is it so certain?' Dr Priestley asked.

'Because the three attempts to murder him must have been carried out by some member of his household. Or two of them, at all events. I can't quite make out that shooting business at present. Just look at the facts. A bottle of poisoned olives was put in his study. The tin of inhalant, kept in his bedroom, was emptied and refilled with this compound of chalk and zinc.

'That limits our search for the criminal at the outset. He or she must have been very intimate with Pershore to know all the necessary details. That he was in the habit of taking an olive every night with his medicine. The exact brand of olives which he preferred. Where they were kept. That Pershore was in the habit of using this particular inhalant for his cough. Where that was kept. And, in addition to this knowledge, the criminal must have had access to both the study and the bedroom, under the watchful eyes of Mrs Markle and the servants. Who but somebody actually living in the house could fulfil all these conditions?'

But Dr Priestley made no reply, and, after a pause, the superintendent continued.

'Now, we have to consider the question of motive. Mrs Markle certainly gains an annuity of not less than two hundred a year by Pershore's death. But I have formed the impression that she was genuinely attached to her employer, in her undemonstrative way. And she was certainly getting two hundred a year, or its equivalent in board and lodging, as things were. The servants had nothing to gain. They may have small legacies, but they have lost very soft and comfortable jobs.

'Who else is there? The nephew, Bryant. He didn't actually live in the house, but I gather he was there pretty often. He certainly spent Sunday afternoon and evening there. But he wasn't there during the preceding week, and the poisoned olives were put in the study before Sunday. The Home Office report proves that. It says that the arsenic was taken over a period of three or four days.

'I thought that Bryant's manner was a bit strange on Monday evening. He cleared out without giving me a chance to talk to him. But at least he didn't disappear altogether. He turned up at the inquest, and talked to me quite reasonably afterwards. Besides, he doesn't stand to make much, if anything, out of his uncle's death.

'Remains Miss Rissington. She spent most of her time at Firlands, and was there until the day of her uncle's death. She had a better opportunity than anybody of monkeying with the olives and the inhalant. With the disappearance of Pershore she is not only freed from irksome restrictions, but she becomes a rich woman. And, finally, she vanishes into space, just when she is most needed.'

'Then you think that Miss Rissington is guilty of her uncle's death?' Dr Priestley remarked.

'It depends what you mean by that exactly, professor. We don't know yet how Pershore was actually killed. But

I believe that she is guilty of two attempts to murder him. And I think she had accomplices, the Sulgraves, probably.'

'And how do you account for the events of Saturday evening?'

'That's a bit of a puzzle. I thought at first that Sulgrave must have fired the shot. But it's now established beyond a doubt that he was at Olympia at the time. Now I'm rather inclined to think that it must have been Mrs Sulgrave, or even Miss Rissington herself. The only thing against that is that women don't usually favour a gun as a weapon.

'I'm pretty sure, as I said last night, that Pershore knew who did it. Why else should he go to all that trouble to conceal the fact that he had been shot at? I haven't a doubt that he put his trousers and pants in the incinerator on Sunday morning, and burnt them, to destroy all traces.'

'You have formed no theory as to what he was doing in the garden at that time of night?'

'I think he was only passing through the garden, on his way to the house from that door into the lane. He had arranged matters so that he could go to and from the house unobserved. I don't know why, but there are dozens of possible explanations. For instance, he may have been in the habit of frequenting the local pub, and he didn't want Mrs Markle and the servants to know it.

'He certainly can't have been out long. Mrs Markle tells me that being alone on Saturday evening he finished dinner early, by a quarter-past eight, and then went to his study. She heard the shot fired soon after nine, and saw him a few minutes later. I've sent a message to the local police, asking them to inquire if anyone saw him about the town during that interval.'

'You do not think it possible that he may have made an appointment with somebody in the garden?'

'I've thought of that. But, look here, professor, that involves a whole lot of unlikely things. He isn't likely to have made a secret appointment like that with any of the people we know. It must have been with somebody who hasn't yet appeared on the scene. Since it was a secret appointment, nobody would know of it but the other party. Then that party must have shot him.'

Dr Priestley smiled. 'It is not easy to pick one's way through your somewhat involved reasoning, superintendent,' he said. 'What is your objection to Mr Pershore having been shot by the other party to the appointment?'

'Why, just this, that it introduces yet another person with a motive for murdering him. And that seems to me utterly unreasonable.'

'I still think that you have misunderstood the reason why that shot was fired,' said Dr Priestley. 'However, in the absence of further facts, you are entitled to your own views. How do you intend to proceed?'

'I'm not going to take any definite action until after tomorrow. At half-past two the funeral is to take place. Bryant, who is representing the family, has arranged for the body to be buried at Weybridge, as you may have seen by the notice in the papers this morning. I'm going to attend it, because I'm rather anxious to see who turns up.'

Dr Priestley seemed to think this was a good idea. Hanslet, by discreet questioning, tried to find out whether he had formed any theory to account for Mr Pershore's death, but without success. Finding his host thus uncommunicative, he said good-night and went home to bed.

Next day he called at Firlands for Mrs Markle, and took

her to the cemetery. They stood just inside the gate, where they could see the mourners as they arrived. Shortly before half-past two, a car drove up. A tall, heavy-featured man of about forty, and a woman some years younger, with a doll-like face got out of it. They were both dressed in black, and had obviously come to attend the ceremony.

At the sight of them, Mrs Markle drew back behind a projecting wall. 'Well, I never!' she exclaimed. 'That's Mr and Mrs Chantley.'

Hanslet remembered the name, and Mrs Markle's apparent reluctance on a previous occasion to discuss these people. 'Didn't you expect them to come?' he asked. 'You told me that they were friends of Mr Pershore, didn't you?'

Again he fancied that there was a curious hesitancy in her manner. 'Oh, yes, friends, of course. That is, they used to be. But Mr Chantley and Mr Pershore haven't seen much of one another recently. I didn't somehow expect they would be here today.'

Any further questions that Hanslet might have put were interrupted by fresh arrivals. Mrs Markle identified them by name. Two of Mr Pershore's colleagues from the office. Doctor Formby. The domestic staff from Firlands. A dozen or so neighbours. And finally the hearse, which had driven down straight from the mortuary, and a single car following it.

From the car descended an elderly gentleman, whom Mrs Markle identified as Mr Judson, the lawyer who had drawn up Mr Pershore's will. He was followed by Philip Bryant, and a rather ill-tempered looking woman, his wife. The procession began to move towards the grave, Mrs Markle and the superintendent keeping well in the rear.

They had nearly reached their destination, when a sound

of hurried footsteps behind them made them look round. An elderly man, short, stout, and very red in the face, had entered the cemetery, and was doing his best to catch up with the mourners. Mrs Markle gave a sudden start. 'Why, it's Mr Hardisen!' she exclaimed.

The newcomer was close enough to hear her. 'So it is, Nancy,' he replied. 'Startled you, eh? Didn't expect to see me, did you? Well, had to see the last of old Nahum. Silly old blighter.' He stared at the superintendent. 'Who's your boy friend?'

'This is Superintendent Hanslet, of Scotland Yard,' she replied.

Hardisen nodded, with an air of complete understanding. 'I thought as much. Something fishy about it, eh? Could tell that, by the inquest. Queer things do happen, we all know. Where's Betty? Don't see her.'

Mrs Markle seemed at a loss for an answer. By this time the rest of the mourners had reached the grave, and Hanslet saw his opportunity. 'We'd better reserve our conversation until the funeral is over,' he said.

They moved on to the graveside, and listened reverently as Mr Pershore's body was committed to the earth. The superintendent remained beside Hardisen, and at the conclusion of the ceremony the two walked to Firlands together.

Hanslet had no intention of wasting his opportunity. 'You were a friend of Mr Pershore's,' he asked tentatively.

Hardisen grunted. '*Was* a friend?' he replied. 'You're right there. I dare say I'm his oldest friend still living. Except perhaps Nancy. Mrs Markle, you know. Can't think why he never married her. Long ago. I remember them both as children. And their parents. Knew them all. Never thought I'd outlive Nahum. He was fifteen years younger than I am. Wouldn't take me for seventy, eh, Mr Hanslet?'

The superintendent glanced at his companion striding along easily at his side. 'You are very well-preserved for your years, if I may say so, Mr Hardisen,' he said.

'Vintage port. That's the secret. Keep any man fit, if he drinks enough of it. Yes, knew them all. Nahum and his two sisters. Aye, further back than that. Old Pershore's first wife, and their son Micah. Must write and tell Micah about this, when I get home.'

'Mr Pershore's half-brother is still alive, then?' asked Hanslet. Somehow it had never occurred to him that this might be the case. He had regarded Micah Pershore as a shadowy figure, long passed into oblivion.

'Still alive? Why shouldn't he be? Same age as I am, almost to a day. Hadn't my constitution, though. Alive when I last heard of him, for all that. Six months ago, that was. He's in the Argentine. Something to do with chilled beef. Made a pot of money, too. Always kept in touch with me. Only person in England he wrote to. Queer chap, Micah. Wouldn't have anything to do with his family. Cleared out soon after Nahum was born. Couldn't abide his step-mother. Don't blame him. Never liked her myself.'

But Hanslet's momentary interest in Micah Pershore evaporated as soon as he learnt that he was in the Argentine. Hardisen himself was a more immediate problem. How was it that the man whom Pershore had stigmatised as a 'damned scoundrel' had come to his funeral? And described himself as his oldest friend, into the bargain?

'Have you seen much of Mr Pershore lately?' he asked.

'No, that I haven't!' replied Hardisen emphatically. 'You never knew Nahum? No? Hot-tempered blighter. Quarrelsome, like his mother. He took after her. The girls didn't. And now all three of them are dead!'

'There was some difference of opinion between you and Mr Pershore, I believe?' said Hanslet. 'Over a loan, was it not?'

Hardisen looked up at him, with a disconcerting grin. 'Smart, you chaps, aren't you?' he replied. 'You've been asking questions. Let's see, now. It wouldn't be Nancy. She's no gossip. Nor yet Betty. Nahum wouldn't have told her. I know! Philip! Don't like Philip. Too smug, by half.'

'There was a misunderstanding between you, was there not?' Hanslet persisted.

'Quite right. Damn silly business. Dare say I was partly to blame. Didn't take Nahum the right way. Ought to have kowtowed to him. But why the devil should I? He chose to be offensive. Oh, well, he's gone, poor old chap. I'm confoundedly sorry it ever happened, now.'

'And, in consequence of this misunderstanding, you and Mr Pershore did not meet?'

'Not for months. We'd only have been rude to one another if we had. But I can't understand his death. So infernally sudden. And he looked fit enough when I saw him.'

'When did you last see him, Mr Hardisen?'

Again Mr Hardisen looked up sharply. 'You don't know that, then?' he replied. 'Why, at the Motor Show, last Monday.'

So unexpected was this statement, that it almost took Hanslet's breath away. He was about to ask for further particulars, when he found that Mrs Markle had joined them. They had reached the gate of Firlands. 'You would like to come in and hear the will read, Mr Hardisen?' she asked.

'Don't mind if I do,' he replied. 'Mr Hanslet coming too? I thought so. Lead on, Nancy.'

They entered the house and made their way to the drawing-room where a small company gradually assembled. Philip Bryant and his wife, Mr Judson, Mrs Rugg and Kate, Mrs Markle, Hardisen, and the superintendent. The remainder of the mourners had gone their respective ways immediately after the funeral.

After a few minutes of rather strained conversation, Mr Judson opened an attache case he had brought with him, and produced the will. He whispered to Philip, who nodded. Then he stood up, cleared his throat, and proceeded to read the document.

Its provisions were those which Philip had already outlined to Hanslet. The principal beneficiary was Betty Rissington, who was left the sum of fifty thousand pounds, free of estate duty. The mortgage on High Elms was cancelled. Mrs Markle was assured of an annuity of two hundred a year. The servants all came in for small legacies. The remainder of the estate fell to Philip Bryant absolutely.

Having finished the reading of the will, Mr Judson once more cleared his throat. He felt it his duty to explain the situation clearly to his hearers. It was doubtful, very doubtful, he might say, whether, after payment of estate duty, the estate would realise sufficient to meet the provisions of the will in full. He had had the opportunity of discussing this matter with the residuary legatee, Mr Philip Bryant. Mr Bryant had adopted a very generous attitude, very generous indeed. He was particularly anxious that his uncle's wishes should be carried out in their entirety. He had therefore undertaken that, in the event of the estate not realising sufficient to meet all the legacies in full, he would provide the additional sum necessary to do so out of his own pocket.

Hanslet caught a venomous glance directed by Mrs Bryant at her husband. Obviously Philip's generous offer had been made without consultation with her. But from the rest of the audience came a murmur of approving gratitude. Hanslet caught Hardisen's eye and the two slipped from the room.

'What's Philip's little game?' Hardisen demanded, as soon as the door was closed behind them.

'I don't know,' replied the superintendent shortly. 'It's none of my business. Now, look here, Mr Hardisen. I want to know all about your meeting with Mr Pershore at the Motor Show.'

'Meeting? It wasn't a meeting. Just caught sight of him. That's all. He didn't see me. Or, if he did, he pretended not to. Walked straight past me. We didn't speak.'

'What were you doing at the Motor Show, Mr Hardisen?'

'What was I doing? What do people do at the Motor Show? Looking round. May buy a new car one of these days. Didn't expect to see Nahum there. Didn't like cars. Wouldn't go in one, if he could help it.'

'What time was it when you saw him?'

'Getting on for two. Waiting for a chance to get lunch. Terrible crush in the dining-room. Standing outside the door. Saw Nahum come out. Passed close by me. He'd had lunch. Anyone could see that.'

'What did you do then?'

'Went in to lunch. Didn't get out till three. Wandered round for a bit. Didn't see Nahum again. Then went home. Six o'clock from Paddington.'

'Was Mr Pershore alone when you saw him?'

'Hadn't got anybody with him, if that's what you mean. Can't call anybody alone at the Motor Show. Hardly room to turn round.'

'Did you visit the stand of Comet Cars Ltd, Number 1001?'

'Saw it in the distance. Didn't go there. Too many people. Might have looked up young George Sulgrave, though. Not a bad fellow in his way. Knew his father very well. Lucky chap, George. His house is his own now. Might have turned up at the funeral. Too busy, I suppose. Could have sent his wife, though. Ever met Irene? Pretty girl. Great friend of Betty's. Where is Betty? Must see her while I'm here.'

Once more Hanslet evaded the question. 'Look here, Mr Hardisen, there are several questions I should like to ask you,' he said. 'As Mr Pershore's oldest friend, you can tell me a lot about him I don't know. Shall we go and have a quiet chat in the study?'

'As you like,' Hardisen replied. 'Doesn't matter, now Nahum's dead. Couldn't do it if he was alive. Hated anyone going there. Come along.'

There was no fire in the study, and it was cold and cheerless. But they made themselves as comfortable as they could, and Hanslet set to work. He had taken a fancy to Hardisen, and decided to confide in him, up to a point.

'The first thing I want to ask you, Mr Hardisen, is this,' he said. 'Do you think that either Mr or Mrs Sulgrave knew that the mortgage on High Elms was to be cancelled on Mr Pershore's death?'

'Probably. Can't say for certain. I didn't know. Nothing to do with me. No reason for Nahum to say anything. Betty knew, no doubt. He told her pretty well everything.

Betty's sure to have told Irene. Bosom friends. Great secret. Eh?'

'Did you know that Mr Pershore was in the habit of taking a dose of medicine, and eating an olive afterwards, every night before he went to bed?'

'Yes. Knew that. Nahum told me. Silly fad. Much better have drunk port.'

'You say you read the account of the inquest. There was arsenic found in the body, you will remember. I was able to trace where that came from. The olives, which were kept in a cupboard in this room, had been poisoned.'

Hardisen looked at him narrowly. 'Who did that?' he asked.

'Wait a minute. Did you know that Mr Pershore used some stuff called Hewart's Inhalant, to stop a cough at night?'

'Didn't know that. Another fad. Nahum loved patent medicines. Better have spent his money on good wine. Done him more good. Well?'

'A mixture had been substituted for that inhalant, which gave off carbon monoxide instead of medicinal vapours. Hence the traces of carbon monoxide mentioned at the inquest.'

Hardisen frowned. 'Dirty tricks,' he exclaimed. And then he looked at the superintendent with a slow light of understanding in his eyes. 'I quarrelled with Nahum. Or rather, he quarrelled with me. Threatened to take proceedings. Damned insulting letter. I meant to get my own back. Tried to murder him. Is that it?'

'If I thought that you had had anything to do with the olives or the inhalant, I should have warned you before I questioned you, Mr Hardisen. I want you, with your knowledge of Mr Pershore's family and household, to help me find the guilty person.'

'Then you don't suspect me? Glad of that. I wouldn't have tried those games. Poison's not in my line. You ask me who did it? What's your own idea?'

'I have no idea at present. But I'm bound to look at it this way, Mr Hardisen. The people who benefit most by Mr Pershore's death are Miss Rissington and the Sulgraves. Now, both Miss Rissington and Mrs Sulgrave disappeared on Monday morning, and haven't been heard of since.'

Mr Hardisen shook his head, slowly and decidedly. 'Not Betty,' he said. 'You can wipe her off the slate. She's not the sort of girl. Hot-tempered perhaps. Like her uncle. Might jab a hatpin into him. Not poison. No. Wouldn't vouch for Irene. Strange girl, that. Deep. Lot deeper than George. Didn't like Nahum. Don't know why.'

He shut his eyes and for a minute or two appeared to be wrapped in profound thought. Then he opened them suddenly, and peered maliciously at the superintendent. 'When did Betty leave here?' he asked.

'On Monday morning. She went up to London with her uncle. She told him she was going to stay with her aunt, Mrs Capel, near Colchester. But she never intended to do so, for she told Mrs Capel that she would not be with her till the end of the week.'

Mr Hardisen shut his eyes again, and uttered a strange noise, which sounded like a saturnine chuckle. 'Couldn't have been Betty, then,' he murmured. 'See that?'

'No, I'm afraid I don't see it,' Hanslet replied coldly.

'Listen, then. Betty puts out the poison. Arsenic and carbon monoxide. Nasty things, both of them. Sure to be fatal, sooner or later. Then she clears out. Leaves uncle to die. What you call an alibi. That's what you think. Eh?'

'You must admit that the facts suggest something of the kind, Mr Hardisen.'

'I don't admit it. Nothing of the kind. Betty's no fool. Got her head screwed on remarkably straight for a woman. Listen to me. You say she put out the poison. Right. What would she do? Any idiot can see that. Stay here. Look after uncle. Nurse him. Smooth his dying brow. Then, when all's over, destroy the clues. Throw away the poisoned olives. Bury the other stuff. Where would you have been then?'

This was an aspect of the matter which had not occurred to Hanslet. There was, undoubtedly, something in Mr Hardisen's contention. Miss Rissington, if indeed she had attempted murder, would have been well advised to destroy the evidence before her departure. But perhaps, knowing that another attempt was to be made at the Motor Show, she had thought that her own attempts would not come to light. He made no reply to Mr Hardisen, and a long pause ensued, during which each pursued his own train of thought.

It was Hardisen who broke the silence. 'About that inquest,' he said suddenly, without opening his eyes. 'Something else, too, wasn't there? Shot found in his legs? When did that happen? Betty shot him, I suppose. Eh?'

'I have discovered that the shot was fired on Saturday evening, soon after nine o'clock,' Hanslet replied. 'I do not know who fired it. But it is well within the bounds of possibility that it was fired by Miss Rissington or Mrs Sulgrave.'

Again Mr Hardisen emitted that saturnine chuckle. 'It wasn't,' he said shortly.

'I don't know how you can be sure of that,' replied the superintendent. 'Unless, of course, you happen to know who did fire the shot?'

Mr Hardisen opened his eyes. He looked at Hanslet speculatively for a moment or two. And then he grinned, as though he had come to the conclusion that the joke was too good not to be shared.

'I fired it myself,' he said.

CHAPTER VIII

Hanslet leapt out of his chair in his amazement at this bald statement. 'You fired the shot that wounded Mr Pershore!' he exclaimed. 'Is that the truth?'

Of course it couldn't be. The superintendent assured himself of that, as soon as he recovered from his momentary amazement. Hardisen was clearly very fond of Miss Rissington. He saw the mess she had got herself into, and was chivalrously trying to take the blame upon himself. It would be interesting to hear how he accounted for his presence at Weybridge on that occasion.

He seemed not in the least disturbed by Hanslet's manner. 'Truth?' he replied. 'Why shouldn't it be? You didn't know Nahum. I did. Sit down, and I'll tell you.'

Hanslet sat down obediently. 'I'm waiting to hear, Mr Hardisen,' he said.

'Listen, then. I came up from Wells on Saturday morning. Stayed at an hotel I know of. Nice quiet place. Give you the address, if you like. Might find it useful. Brought a twelve-bore up with me. Wanted adjustment. Left it at a

113

gunsmith's in Pall Mall on Monday morning. It's there now.'

'One moment, Mr Hardisen. I'd like the name of the hotel and the gunsmith, if you don't mind.'

Hardisen supplied these particulars without the slightest hesitation. 'Couldn't leave the gun on Saturday,' he continued. 'Shops closed by the time I got up. Left it at the hotel. Went to the Motor Show. Too crowded for comfort. Came away. Found myself at a loose end. Nothing to do. Thought I'd come down here. Meant to take a rise out of Nahum.'

'What exactly do you mean by that?' Hanslet asked.

'Just going to tell you. Nahum had been devilish offensive. All over nothing. Could have had his thousand back. If he'd asked properly, that is. Wouldn't have hurt me. Wrote out a cheque yesterday. Soon as I saw the notice of his death. Got it on me now. Here it is. Look!'

He produced from his pocket a cheque for one thousand pounds, made out in favour of Mr Pershore's executors, and brandished it in the superintendent's face. 'Nahum could have had it,' he continued. 'Only had to ask for it. Decently, of course. But not he. What does he do? Goes to that ass Philip. Tells him to write me threatening letters. Finally writes himself. Tells me he's instituted proceedings. Says he'll make my name mud. Ruin my business. Send me to the workhouse. Dance on my grave. Look down from Abraham's bosom. Watch me writhing in hell. Ever read your Bible?'

'Sometimes,' Hanslet replied. 'Did he really use those expressions?'

'Plenty others besides. That was last week. Still got the letter. Having it framed. Shan't do that now, though. All forgiven and forgotten. Still, you can see it.'

'I should like to do so. You were indignant when you received that letter?'

'Indignant? Good word, that. Dancing mad. That's more like it. Bit irritable myself. Mightn't think it, to look at me. It's vintage port, that's what it is.'

Whether vintage port was responsible for Mr Hardisen's irritability, or for his benign appearance, Hanslet was left to guess. The other continued, in his staccato style, before he had time to put the question.

'Wasn't going to stand that. Couldn't expect me to. Wrote to Nahum. Tore up the letter. Not abusive enough. Wanted time to think. Came up to London on Saturday. Still thinking. Thought of several things. Really nasty. Wanted to make him sit up. Then the idea came.'

'What idea?' asked Hanslet.

'How to get my own back. Frighten him. Better than writing. Nahum was a coward. Always had been. Even as a boy. Run away if anyone chucked a stone at him. Wouldn't say boo to a goose. Let alone a gander. Afraid it might bite him. Ah, well, he's gone now.'

Mr Hardisen closed his eyes once more. He was silent so long that Hanslet fancied he had gone to sleep. 'So you decided to give Mr Pershore a fright?' he said.

'That's right,' murmured Mr Hardisen, as though from the depths of a dream. 'Give him a fright. Startle the wits out of him. Make him think his precious skin was in danger. That was the idea that came to me. On the way back from the Motor Show. Damn silly. See that now.'

He opened his eyes and stared pessimistically at the unlighted fire. Then he felt in his pockets, found a match, struck it, and put it to the paper. 'That's better,' he said. 'Devilish cold in here. Nahum wouldn't mind. Never

115

grudged fuel. Cost will fall on Philip now. He won't be so pleased. Stingy devil, Philip. What's his game, eh? Tell me that!'

But Hanslet was not to be led away from the original subject. 'I want you to tell me exactly what you did on Saturday evening, after you had decided to give Mr Pershore a fright,' he said firmly.

'What I did?' Mr Hardisen replied. 'Dined early. Half-past six. Against all my principles. Never done such a thing before. Won't again. Couldn't enjoy my glass of port. Went and got the gun. Taxi to Waterloo. Train down here. Half-past eight when I arrived at the station. Thought I'd walk round by the back lane. Less chance of being seen.'

'Did you expect to find Mr Pershore in the garden?'

'Not I. Not on a cold night like that. Expected Nahum would be asleep after dinner. In this very chair I'm sitting in now. Meant to walk in at the front gate. Creep round the house. Knock on the window. Wake Nahum. He'd draw the curtain. See me. I'd point the gun at him. Then fire it in the air. He'd think he was shot. Frighten him to death. Meanwhile I clear off. Damn fool idea.'

Hanslet smiled, in spite of himself. This old boy was certainly a character, he thought. 'But you didn't carry out your scheme?' he said.

Mr Hardisen shook his head. 'Hadn't a chance. Got to the end of the lane. Found a car there. Small Comet saloon. Nobody in it. Lights out. Thought this queer. Walked up the lane. Far as the gate leading into the garden. Heard voices. Other side of the paling. Recognised Nahum's. Other was a woman's. Didn't know it.'

He leant forward, picked up the poker, and very cautiously lifted the fire. 'Badly laid,' he growled. 'Just like women. Never can lay a fire properly. That's better. Couldn't make out that voice. Wasn't Betty's. Wasn't Nancy's. Seemed to me I'd heard it before. Didn't know what to do. Went a few steps up the lane. Then the door opened. Drat that fire!'

'Never mind the fire, Mr Hardisen,' said Hanslet impatiently. 'It'll burn up all right in a minute. The door in the paling opened. What happened then?'

'Woman came out. All muffled up. Moonlight night, but dark in the lane. Couldn't recognise her. Door shut again. She started up the lane. Towards the car. Didn't see me. Not for the moment. Not till I sneezed. That startled her!' And he chuckled heartily at the recollection of the scene.

'You seem to have frightened more than one person that night, Mr Hardisen. What did the woman do when you sneezed?'

'Looked round. Caught sight of me. With the gun. Couldn't tell who it was. Not in that light. Sort of gasped. Took to her heels. Towards the car. I let her go. Couldn't be bothered with her. It was Nahum I was after. He was my bird.'

'Where was Mr Pershore all this time?' Hanslet asked.

'Other side of the paling. There's a gap by the door. One of the slats gone. Looked through that. Saw Nahum walking up the garden. Towards the house. Hadn't heard me sneeze. Or thought it was the woman. Saw him quite plain. In the moonlight. Waited a bit. Didn't want to kill him Just pepper him a bit. That's all.'

'Very humane of you, Mr Hardisen. You waited until he was some distance away?'

'That's right. Watched him go up the path. Put the gun

through the gap. Aimed at his backside. Pulled the trigger. Bang! Just like that. Poor old Nahum! Fool trick.'

'It was a fool trick,' said Hanslet, with as much gravity as he could muster. 'What did you do then?'

'Saw Nahum jump. Just like a rabbit. Then make tracks. Up towards the house. Heard a yell from the woman. Car started up. Drove off like hell. Thought she'd gone for the cops. Time I cleared out. Walked back to the station. Caught a train to Waterloo. Then to my hotel. Cleaned the gun. Went to bed. Slept like a log.'

Mr Hardisen obviously considered this to be the end of the story. He lay back in his chair, closed his eyes, and folded his hands contentedly over his stomach.

The superintendent frowned at him for a moment or two in silent disapproval. His manner left no room for doubt that he was telling the truth. So picturesque an account could not have been the fruit of his unaided imagination. But had he told the whole truth? Hanslet doubted it. 'It seems to me, Mr Hardisen, that there's only one thing for me to do,' he said sharply.

'What's that?' Hardisen replied, in a sleepy voice.

'Why, to arrest you on a charge of unlawful wounding.'

Hardisen shook his head slowly. 'No go!' he replied without opening his eyes. 'Couldn't prove it. Where are your witnesses? Nahum's dead. Lady won't show up. Not she. Needn't fret about that. What was she doing here? Answer me that!'

'I could charge you on your own confession, you know.'

'All right. Go ahead. Put me in court. In front of the beak. What do I say? Sorry, your Worship. Not guilty. Superintendent's a lamb. Child could play with him. But a bit too credulous. All a fairy story. Simple tales for simple 'tecs. Where'd you be then? Beak furious. Wasting his time. Prisoner discharged. No stain on his character. Police look silly. Eh?'

'Look here, Mr Hardisen. I'd be glad if you'd be serious!' exclaimed Hanslet angrily. 'Is this story the truth, or is it not?'

'That depends,' Hardisen murmured. 'Arrest, you said. What about it?'

There was something so ludicrous about the situation that Hanslet laughed aloud. Quite clearly Hardisen was not a man to be moved by threats. But already he had shown signs of responding to gentle treatment. 'All right, Mr Hardisen,' he said. 'We won't say anything more about arrest. You did a very silly thing, as you admit yourself, but I think we can afford to overlook it. Now, entirely between ourselves, as man to man. Is what you have just told me the truth, or is it merely a fairy story?'

'That's better. Shouldn't care to be arrested. Confounded nuisance. You've had the truth. Word of honour.'

'Well, it's a lucky thing that you didn't damage Mr Pershore more than you did. Naturally, in the light of what has happened, I'm particularly interested in the woman you saw that night. You are quite sure that you didn't recognise her?'

'Quite sure. Never saw her face. Pretty dark, remember. Young woman, could tell that. Nothing more. Ran like a deer.'

'You are quite sure that it was not Miss Rissington?'

'Betty? No, it wasn't Betty. Not her voice. Not her shape. Stouter. Not so long in the limb. Should have known Betty all right.'

'Could it have been Mrs Sulgrave?'

'Irene? Don't think so. Not her voice, either. Haven't seen Irene lately. Not for months. Couldn't swear to her in the dark.'

'But you hadn't seen Miss Rissington for months, either,' Hanslet objected.

Hardisen chuckled. 'Haven't I?' he replied. 'Who said so?'

'Mrs Markle told me that you haven't been here since the beginning of the year.'

'Quite true. Nancy's like that. Never told a lie. Not in her life. But I've seen Betty. Managed that all right. Great pals, Betty and I. Came to stay with me. Down at Wells. Last month. Nahum didn't know. Thought she was with Aunt Chloe. Mrs Capel, you know. Quite proper. No scandal. Got a housekeeper. Regular tigress. Devoted to Betty, though. Betty didn't know. About Nahum and me, I mean. Couldn't make out why we had quarrelled. Pestered me with questions. Wouldn't tell her. Said she'd ask her uncle.'

'She did,' said Hanslet grimly. 'And in reply she was told that you were a damned scoundrel.'

This brought on another of Hardisen's chuckling fits. 'Good old Nahum,' he spluttered. 'Can't have been in form that day. Should have expected something stronger. Didn't want to shock Betty. Must have been that.'

'So Miss Rissington was staying with you last month, was she?' said Hanslet thoughtfully. 'Now, look here, Mr Hardisen. I've got to find her, and I shall have to put the police on the job, unless I can find out by some other means where she is. You seem to have been in her confidence. Can't you make any suggestion as to where she may have got to?'

'I might. Not going to, though. Can't trust you. You'd have her arrested. Something damn silly like that. She's innocent. Every fool knows it.'

'She may be innocent, Mr Hardisen. But you must admit that her sudden disappearance looks a bit suspicious.'

'Suspicious? Nonsense! Look here. Tell you what I'll do. I can guess where she may be. What will you do to her? If you get hold of her, that is?'

'I shan't do anything drastic, you needn't be afraid of that. I merely want to question her.'

'Third degree, eh? Not on your life. I'll make a bargain, though. Somebody else must be present. While you question her. Ought to be a solicitor. Don't trust Philip. What about me, eh?'

Hanslet considered this for a minute. He would rather have tackled Miss Rissington alone, or in the presence of another police officer. But, after all, Hardisen's presence could not very greatly complicate matters. 'I have no objection to that,' he replied. 'On condition that you will tell me where to find her, of course.'

'Shan't do that. Betty shall judge for herself. I'll do this. Stay in London tonight. Send her a wire. Put the position up to her. Leave it to her. Come back or not as she likes. I know she'll come. Right away. If so, I'll tell you. See her together. Is that a bargain?'

'That's a bargain, Mr Hardisen,' replied Hanslet promptly.

Hardisen opened one eye, glanced at the superintendent, and shut it again. 'I know what you're thinking,' he murmured. 'Trace the wire. Find out that way. Nothing doing.'

As a matter of fact, that was exactly what Hanslet had thought. This man Hardisen was a good deal more subtle than his appearance suggested. 'You must remember that I am a policeman, and must do my duty,' he replied.

'Right. Most praiseworthy sentiment. Do your duty. Arrest me. Unlawful wounding. That's what you called it. Silly phrase. What's lawful wounding? Tell me that!'

Hanslet capitulated with a shrug of the shoulders. 'I haven't the slightest intention of arresting you, Mr Hardisen. And, if you will be good enough to send a wire to the address which you think will find Miss Rissington, I will undertake not to make any attempt to trace that wire for twenty-four hours from now. Will that satisfy you?'

This time Hardisen opened both eyes. 'Honest Injun?' he asked.

'I give you my solemn word.'

His scrutiny of the superintendent's face seemed to satisfy Hardisen. 'I'll trust you,' he said 'You look honest. For a policeman. Betty's innocent. That's why I'm doing this. Wouldn't if I wasn't sure of it. Keep your eye on Philip. What's his game?'

The constant reiteration of this question was beginning to arouse Hanslet's suspicions. Hardisen openly proclaimed his dislike of Philip Bryant, and his affection for Miss Rissington. It was only natural that he should try to put Philip forward as a scapegoat in the place of his protegée. 'Why do you suggest that I should keep my eye on Mr Bryant?' the superintendent asked lightly.

'Because he's not to be trusted,' Mr Hardisen replied. 'Slippery customer. Always was. So was his father. Sharp as a needle. Philip's mean. Never spends a penny. Not if a halfpenny will do instead. Why has he made this offer? About the estate, I mean?'

'He doesn't want any of the beneficiaries to suffer, I suppose. It seems to me to be very generous behaviour on his part.'

'Nonsense. All eyewash. You mark my words. He knows the position. You can bet your shirt on that. He won't have to put his hand in his pocket. The estate will realise enough. More than enough. Like to bet on it?'

'No, I'm not a betting man,' Hanslet replied. 'If you've no more against Mr Bryant than that, I needn't waste my time keeping an eye on him.'

'Please yourself. Your job to find out who killed Nahum. Not mine. Glad of that.'

'Well, Mr Bryant can't have had any hand in that,' said Hanslet, in a tone of complete conviction. 'He had nothing on earth to gain by his uncle's death. In fact, he looks like losing by it.'

'Don't you be so sure. Philip won't lose. Not the sort that does. He'll manage to profit somewhere. Staying down here?'

The abruptness of the question startled Hanslet. 'No, I'm going back to London at once.'

'I'll come with you. Send that wire. You're to be found at the Yard, eh?'

'If I'm not there, they'll tell you where I am, or send me a message.'

'Good. Let's slip away quietly. Don't want to see Philip, or his wife. You ready?'

Hanslet nodded, and they left the house. Together they walked to the station, and took a train to Waterloo, where they separated.

The superintendent spent the rest of the evening at Scotland Yard, making certain inquiries by telephone. This occupied him until eight o'clock, by which time no message had reached him from Hardisen. He informed his subordinates where he was to be found, if this message should come, then went out in search of a meal. When he had finished, he went to Westbourne Terrace to report progress to Dr Priestley.

He found that he was not the only visitor, for Doctor Oldland had dropped in a few minutes earlier. Dr Priestley welcomed him as though he had expected him. 'Well, superintendent,' he said. 'Did you attend the funeral?'

'Yes, and I'm very glad I thought of it,' Hanslet replied. 'I made the acquaintance of a very remarkable character, and learned quite a lot from him.'

'That is very satisfactory,' said Dr Priestley. 'Who is this remarkable character?'

'Mr Hardisen, from Wells. The old friend with whom Mr Pershore had quarrelled.'

'And whom he described as a "Damned scoundrel?"' Doctor Oldland inquired.

'That's the chap. I had the most amazing conversation with him. I'd like to repeat it to you, Professor, if you've the patience to listen.'

Dr Priestley nodded, and Harold Merefield, who was present, prepared to take notes. Hanslet thus encouraged, repeated, in rather less picturesque language, what Mr Hardisen had told him.

Oldland was immensely amused at the recital. 'It seems to me that your friend is a pretty shrewd customer,' he said. 'Do you suppose that he was telling the truth?'

'His statements are correct, as far as I have been able to check them. He stayed at the hotel he mentioned on Saturday and Sunday nights. He left there, carrying a gun, about seven on Saturday evening, and returned, still with the gun, about half-past ten. He left the gun with the gunsmith whose name he gave me, on Monday morning.'

'Well, it's one of the queerest things I ever heard,' said Oldland. 'I don't quite understand why he came out with the whole story, on such short acquaintance.'

'I think I do. His principal idea is to shield Miss Rissington, of whom he seems very fond. I rather gave him the impression that I suspected her of having fired the shot. Anyway, that little problem is cleared up. For the rest, he did his best to divert my suspicions from Miss Rissington by throwing out dark hints against Bryant. I tried to draw him out, by appearing to be convinced of Bryant's innocence, but I wasn't very successful.'

'Mr Hardisen made one great point in Miss Rissington's favour,' Dr Priestley remarked. 'It is the natural instinct of the murderer to destroy incriminating evidence, as he pointed out. I agree with him that if Miss Rissington were guilty, she would almost certainly have done so before her departure.'

'Well, that's as may be, Professor. There may be some simple explanation for her failure to do so. You must admit that nobody else had her opportunities, or so much to gain by her uncle's death. For the moment, I'm more interested in the woman who was with Pershore on Saturday evening. Who was she, and what was she doing?'

'It wasn't Miss Rissington,' said Oldland positively. 'If it had been, Hardisen would have recognised her. And, if he had, he wouldn't have mentioned the presence of a woman at all. That's a pretty sound argument, isn't it, Priestley?'

'Yes, I think that is a reasonable assumption,' Dr Priestley replied.

'Then if it wasn't Miss Rissington, it was Mrs Sulgrave,' said Hanslet. 'The two were working hand in glove, I'm sure of that. I was making inquiries just now, and I've found out that Mrs Sulgrave has a small Comet saloon of her own. That was the car Hardisen saw, no doubt.'

'You can't be certain of that,' Oldland replied. 'There are a lot of those small Comet saloons about. The Comet people made a great feature of them during the last couple of years. Whether they'll sell so many, now that they've adopted this new-fangled transmission, I rather doubt.'

'Speculation, in the absence of definite facts, is apt to be unprofitable,' said Dr Priestley acidly. 'There is another aspect of the matter which seems to have escaped your attention, superintendent. How did this woman obtain access to the garden of Firlands?'

'Why, Pershore must have been expecting her, and let her in by the door leading on to the lane.'

'Not necessarily. She may have left the car where Mr Hardisen saw it, and walked round to the front entrance. From there she could have reached the back of the house unobserved, as Mr Hardisen himself intended to do, and tapped on the study window to attract Mr Pershore's attention. It does not follow that he expected her visit.'

'All the more reason that she should have been Mrs Sulgrave. She knew her way about the place, since she goes there pretty frequently. And Hardisen couldn't say definitely that it wasn't Mrs Sulgrave.'

'I am not denying the possibility that this woman was Mrs Sulgrave. I am endeavouring to point out that you cannot assume the fact without further evidence.'

'I don't see who else it can have been, Professor,' Hanslet replied obstinately. 'You must remember that Miss

Rissington was dining with Mrs Sulgrave that evening. This, I imagine, is pretty much what happened. Miss Rissington reported that neither the olives nor the inhalant seemed to be having any effect. They hit upon some scheme whereby, if Pershore could be enticed to the Motor Show, he could be finished off there. What that scheme was, I haven't yet discovered.

'The point was, how was he to be enticed there? Perhaps, if Sulgrave were to send him a ticket, with a personal request to visit the Comet stand, he would consent to go. Better still, if Mrs Sulgrave used her powers of persuasion. So Mrs Sulgrave jumps into the car, and goes straight off to put it to Pershore.'

Dr Priestley shook his head. 'I admire the ingenuity of your theory, superintendent,' he said. 'But it appears to possess one grave flaw. Why, if Mrs Sulgrave's errand was so apparently innocent, should she not have driven up to the front door, rang the bell, and asked to see Mr Pershore in the ordinary way?'

'I suppose because she didn't want anybody else to know she had seen him,' Hanslet replied, rather lamely.

'She could not ensure that he would not mention her visit. To Mrs Markle, for instance. No, I think it more probable that the interview between Mr Pershore and his visitor was of a definitely clandestine nature. But it need not have had any connection with his death, or with the previous attempts upon his life.'

'You may be right, Professor. But I can't get away from the idea that it was Mrs Sulgrave. Anybody else, on hearing the shot, would surely have informed the police. But this woman doesn't. She merely rings up later and asks if Pershore is all right.'

'You do not know what motives she had for keeping her own counsel. If, as I suspect, the interview was of a clandestine nature, the woman would not wish to reveal her presence at Firlands.'

'I gather, Professor, that you do not altogether favour the theory of a conspiracy between Miss Rissington and the Sulgraves?'

'I reserve my judgment upon that. But it is apparent, I think, that it is not the only possible theory. In my opinion, you have laid too much stress upon the obvious motives contained in the provisions of Mr Pershore's will. Other motives, as yet undiscovered, may have existed.'

'Well, what would you suggest, Professor?'

'I should, were I in your place, widen the field of my inquiries very considerably. I should, for instance, endeavour to secure fuller details of Mr Pershore's life and habits. Mr Hardisen may be able to help you there. And there is Mr Pershore's half-brother, with whom Mr Hardisen apparently corresponded.'

'But, dash it all, Professor, he's in the Argentine!' Hanslet exclaimed.

'He was in the Argentine when Mr Hardisen last heard from him. Do you know for a fact that he is there now? Even if he is, he may have exerted some influence upon Mr Pershore's death.'

Before Hanslet could reply, the telephone bell rang in the hall. Merefield got up to answer it. 'Somebody asking for you, Mr Hanslet,' he said as he returned.

The superintendent went to the instrument. 'Hanslet speaking,' he said. 'Who's that?'

Mr Hardisen's voice replied to him. 'That you, superintendent? Good. Rang up the Yard. Asked where you were.

They gave me a number. Listen to me. Heard from Betty. She'll be at Firlands tomorrow. Ten o'clock in the morning. Meet you there. Good-night.'

And before Hanslet could reply, he had rung off.

CHAPTER IX

Hanslet travelled down to Weybridge next morning in a jubilant frame of mind. He was quite confident of his ability to get at the bottom of things now. This girl, Miss Rissington, would not stand up long under his cross-examination. And as for Mr Hardisen, her self-appointed protector, well, he was pretty shrewd, certainly. But Hanslet had no doubt which would prove the shrewder of the two, if it came to a battle of wits.

He reached Firlands shortly after ten, and was shown into the drawing-room. A moment or two later the door opened again, and a tall fair girl entered, escorted by Mr Hardisen, the top of whose head hardly reached above her shoulder.

She bowed rather stiffly. 'Good-morning, Mr Hanslet,' she said. 'I'm sorry I've given you all this trouble. You want to talk to me, don't you?' She sat down on the arm of a chair, and nodded to Hanslet to find a seat for himself. 'Give me a fag, Uncle Odin, there's a darling,' she continued.

As she helped herself to a cigarette from Mr Hardisen's

case and lighted it, Hanslet observed her narrowly. In spite of a very good figure, she could not be pronounced pretty. Her features were too hard for that. But it was a strong face, the face of a girl who knew her own mind, and who probably would not be afraid of expressing her opinions.

'Yes, I have been anxious to talk to you for some time, Miss Rissington,' replied Hanslet quietly. 'Ever since the sudden death of your uncle, in fact.'

She smiled with her lips, but her eyes remained hard and unwavering. 'Yes, Uncle Odin has told me all about that,' she said. 'Naturally you think that as I am his niece and lived in the house with him, I ought to know something about it. Well, I can assure you I don't. I happened to be crossing the Channel at the time it happened.'

Mr Hardisen had subsided into the chair nearest the fire. From here he fixed the Superintendent with a baleful glare. 'That's right,' he growled. 'Easy to prove it. Perfect alibi.'

'Do you mind telling me the reason for your crossing the Channel on Monday?' Hanslet asked.

'Oh, I'd better tell you all about it, I suppose. I went to stay with some people in Paris. They're Irene's friends, really, but they asked me to come too. And I'm afraid we were having such a gay time that we didn't worry much about the newspapers. I assure you that I knew nothing about Uncle Nahum's death until I got Uncle Odin's wire yesterday evening. I came back at once, of course.'

'Why did you tell your uncle that you were going to stay with Mrs Capel?'

'For a very good reason. Uncle Nahum was a great dear in many ways, but he was terribly narrow-minded, especially about people. If he liked them, I was expected to like them too. If he didn't, he hated me to have anything

131

to do with them. And he took a ridiculous dislike to these friends of mine from the first. He said they had foreign manners, which in his eyes was an unforgivable sin. There would have been awful ructions if I'd told him I was going to stay with them. So I practised a little harmless deception, that's all.'

'I see. Do I understand that Mrs Sulgrave went to Paris with you?'

'Of course. She met me at Victoria on Monday morning. And she came back with me, too.'

'Mrs Sulgrave told her maid that she had gone to look after a friend who had met with an accident in the north of England,' said Hanslet severely.

'I ought to know that, since I sent her the telegram myself,' replied Betty Rissington, with a slight shrug of the shoulders. 'We fixed all that up between us. Nobody would ever have known, if it hadn't been for the accident to Uncle Nahum.'

'A little deception was necessary in Mrs Sulgrave's case as well, then?'

'Only because men have to be treated like children. George doesn't like these friends of hers, either. He thinks the husband is too fond of her. I'm sure he is, for that matter, but Irene is quite capable of looking after herself. Not that George's objections would have stopped her. But she hates a scene, so she just didn't tell him.'

'When did you and Mrs Sulgrave arrange to go to Paris on Monday?'

'Oh, long ago. We purposely fixed it for the time of the Motor Show, for then we knew that George would be staying in London, and wouldn't have time to ask too many questions.'

'You've got it now,' murmured Mr Hardisen, from the depths of the chair. 'What did I tell you? Pretty simple!'

Hanslet disregarded him. 'You travelled up to London with your uncle on Monday morning, Miss Rissington,' he said. 'Did he tell you that he was going to the Motor Show?'

Again she smiled. 'No, he didn't,' she replied. 'He told me that he was going to the office.'

This struck Hanslet as peculiar. Yet she had every appearance of telling the truth. 'Can you think of any reason which would have induced your uncle to visit Olympia?' he asked.

She shrugged her shoulders slightly. 'A good few thousand people find a sufficient reason for going to the Motor Show,' she replied.

'They are presumably interested in cars. Your uncle was not, I believe?'

'He was sometimes interested in people, though. He may have gone to meet somebody there.'

'He met Mr Hardisen there, as it happened,' said Hanslet quietly.

'Eh? What's that?' Hardisen exclaimed. 'Didn't go there to meet me. Rubbish! Didn't even look at me. Told you that before.'

'Yes, I remember you did,' Hanslet replied. 'By the way, Miss Rissington, did Mr Hardisen tell you that on Saturday evening he shot at your uncle and wounded him?'

'Oh, yes, he told me that, just before you came. He and Uncle Nahum were a pair of idiots to behave like that. And I told Uncle Odin that if he'd really hurt him, I'd never have spoken to him again.'

'Quite right!' said Hardisen, with that irritating chuckle

133

of his. 'She told me off properly. Said I was a silly old fool. Perhaps I am. Wish I'd never done it now. Eh, Betty?'

'You ought to be put in prison,' said Betty Rissington severely. But her eyes told him that she forgave him.

Hanslet intercepted the glance, and realised that his attempt to drive a wedge between the allies had failed. 'We're getting away from the point,' he said. 'I have reason to believe that Mr Pershore did, in fact, go to Olympia to meet someone and that that person was Mr Sulgrave.'

'Then why shouldn't he have told me so?' she replied. 'I think it's much more likely that he went there to meet Philip, to talk about something that he didn't want to discuss in his office. How he could best annoy Uncle Odin, for instance.'

'Was Mr Bryant at the Motor Show on Monday?'

'I don't know. Haven't you thought of asking him? All I can tell you is that when Philip was dining here on Sunday evening he said he would go to the Show on Monday afternoon, if he could get away.'

'That's news to me,' said Hardisen. 'Remember what I said. Keep your eye on Philip. He was at the Show, was he? Queer, that.'

But Hanslet was not to be diverted to the subject of Philip Bryant. 'It was a curious fact, in connection with your uncle's death, Miss Rissington, that two previous attempts were made to poison him,' he said.

'Yes, I know. Uncle Odin has told me. I can scarcely believe it. It sounds impossible.'

'Mr Hardisen seems to have had time to tell you a good deal,' said Hanslet irritably. 'What time did you meet him this morning, may I ask?'

'I called for him at his hotel at half-past seven this

134

morning, on my way from Victoria,' she replied sweetly. 'He asked me to do that when he wired me.'

Hanslet turned angrily upon the impassive Hardisen. 'Why did you tell me last night that Miss Rissington would be here at ten o'clock this morning?' he demanded.

'Why not? Perfectly true. She was. You found her here. Wanted first innings. Put her wise. Never said I wouldn't. Kept to my bargain. Can't deny that.'

Before Hanslet could reply, Betty Rissington spoke. 'Don't let's start another quarrel,' she said. 'I'm very grateful to Uncle Odin. He told me of what had happened here, and warned me that you suspected me of trying to poison Uncle Nahum. I can only tell you, on my word of honour, that I didn't, and that I knew nothing about it until this morning.'

'Two definite attempts were made. A bottle of poisoned olives was placed in the cupboard of Mr Pershore's study. A poisonous powder was substituted for the Hewart's Inhalant in his bedroom. Do you mean to tell me that you knew nothing whatever of either of these attempts, Miss Rissington?'

'I have just told you that I did not even hear of them until this morning,' she replied firmly.

'No good bullying the girl,' growled Hardisen. 'She's innocent. Look at her!'

Hanslet was bound to admit to himself that she showed no trace of confusion. But he was not to be put off. 'Mr Hardisen has told you, perhaps, of the provisions of your uncle's will?' he asked.

'He has. But I knew them long ago, at least as far as they concerned me. He always told me that he hoped to leave me fifty thousand pounds when he died. I also knew that he meant to do something for Mrs Markle and the servants. But I knew nothing about the mortgage on George's house. And I don't think that George himself can have known that it was to be cancelled, or he'd have told Irene, and she'd have told me.'

'May I ask what allowance your uncle made to you, Miss Rissington?'

'He allowed me eight hundred a year. And if I couldn't make that do, I had only to ask him for a cheque, and he gave it me at once.'

'Since you know nothing about the olives and the inhalant, perhaps you can suggest somebody who does. Have you any reason to suspect Mrs Markle, or any of the domestic staff?'

'That would be too utterly silly,' she replied tranquilly. 'Even sillier than your idea that I tried to murder Uncle Nahum for his money.'

Hardisen chuckled, but the superintendent affected not to notice him. 'You had access to both the study and Mr Pershore's bedroom?' he asked.

'If by that you mean that I could have gone into them when he was out, I had. But I certainly wasn't in the study for at least ten days before he died. He hated anyone going in there, and the last time I went, he took me in himself, to show me some soot which had fallen down the chimney. Mrs Markle happened to be out, or he would have shown her. I sent Jessie in to sweep it up. He never spoke to the servants himself, if he could help it.'

'Did Mrs Sulgrave go into the study when she was here on Friday last?'

'Irene? Why ever should she? I'm quite certain she didn't, for she was with me all the time she was here.'

'Somebody must have put those poisoned olives in the cupboard, Miss Rissington. Don't you know of anybody who may have entered the study during the week preceding your uncle's death?'

She shook her head. 'I don't know of anybody,' she replied. 'Only Philip. Uncle Nahum took him in there after lunch on Sunday.'

'Philip?' murmured Mr Hardisen. 'Can't get away from Philip. Dark horse. Very. Eh?'

This reiteration of Philip Bryant's name was beginning to get on Hanslet's nerves. Could there be anything in it? Sunday afternoon, after lunch. Bryant had gone into the study with his uncle. Mr Pershore might have dozed off in his chair. Or gone to the lavatory across the passage. Bryant might have seized the opportunity of putting the poisoned olives in the cupboard. But, on second thoughts, that wouldn't do. Only one night had elapsed between then and Mr Pershore's death. Unless he had departed from his usual habits, he would then only have eaten one olive. But the Home Office report suggested that he had eaten at least two, with an interval between them. He had not eaten an olive on Saturday night. Therefore the substitution must have been made on Friday, if not earlier.

'When were you last in Mr Pershore's bedroom, Miss Rissington?' asked Hanslet, after a pause.

'I really don't remember. Not for ages. Not since I bought that vaporiser for him, and showed him how to use it. And that was a long time ago.'

Inquiries in this direction seemed utterly unprofitable. Hanslet was about to start upon a fresh subject, when Mrs Markle appeared, with a message that he was wanted on the telephone.

He went to the instrument, and was informed that Inspector Jarrold wished to speak to him. The inspector's message was brief and to the point. 'Thought you might like to know that Mrs Sulgrave came home to High Elms this morning.'

'Thanks,' Hanslet replied. 'I'll go on there when I've finished here.' He returned to the drawing-room, feeling that the interruption had made it easier for him to broach a new subject. 'I noticed two mourners at your uncle's funeral yesterday, Miss Rissington. Mr and Mrs Chantley. Mrs Markle seemed rather surprised to see them there. Were they friends of Mr Pershore's?'

Betty Rissington glanced at Mr Hardisen before she replied. 'Mr Chantley was his friend at one time. They saw quite a lot of one another. I never liked him much, and I wasn't sorry when he gave up coming here.'

'Do you know why he gave up coming here?'

'People had a way of giving up coming to see Uncle Nahum. He was apt to offend them, without really meaning to. He hated being contradicted, and if anybody persisted in sticking to their own opinions, he used to get cross and rude. I think that's a fair way of putting it, isn't it, Uncle Odin?'

'Fair?' repeated Hardisen. 'Too mild, by half. Nahum wasn't rude. He was damned offensive. Used shocking language. That's the truth.'

'And he offended Mr Chantley?' Hanslet asked.

'I'm sure I don't know,' Betty Rissington replied. 'You'd better ask him. I don't know anything about it, and I didn't ask. I really wasn't interested, as long as I wasn't asked to be nice to Mr Chantley any longer.'

'And Mrs Chantley? You were acquainted with her, of course?'

'Oh, Sonia Chantley is one of those colourless people that one doesn't miss. She's not a bad sort in her way, but she's completely under her husband's thumb. She used to drift along here occasionally to see me. But since her husband and Uncle Nahum parted brass-rags I've never seen her. He told her she wasn't to come, I suppose. And naturally, I have never taken the trouble to look her up.'

'Who are these people, Miss Rissington?'

'He's in business of some kind. They've got quite a nice house in Surbiton. I fancy that they're quite well off. I'm rather surprised that they turned up at the funeral, since we've seen nothing of them for so long.'

'Nothing in that,' said Hardisen. 'Was there myself. Let bygones be bygones. Bury the hatchet in the grave. That's what I thought. Same idea occurred to them.'

Hanslet thought this quite likely. It might be worth while having a word with Chantley. He might be able to throw some light on Pershore's history and habits.

Meanwhile, here was Pershore's niece, who was surely the best authority.

'I'd like to get some idea of how your uncle spent his time, Miss Rissington,' he said.

'He used to go up to London three or four times a week. He would leave here about ten, and get back usually about six. Sometimes he would stay up and dine with friends, but not very often. He had an office in Lambeth, as no doubt you know.'

'What did he do in the days that he did not go up to London?'

'Oh, just pottered about. He hadn't any regular hobby. He used to spend a lot of time in his study. In fact, this autumn, he has spent more time there than anywhere else in the house. I've no idea what he did with himself. Looked at the papers and dozed, I expect. He'd go in there directly after dinner, and not go to bed until after midnight, sometimes.'

'Mr Hardisen told you of his adventure on Saturday evening. Did he mention the fact that there was a woman in the garden here when he arrived on the scene?'

'He did. It's no good asking me who it was, for I haven't the slightest idea.'

'You went to dine at High Elms that evening, did you not, Miss Rissington?'

'Yes. Irene came and fetched me, and drove me home just before one o'clock in the morning. By that time everybody in the house had gone to bed. I never noticed anything wrong with Uncle Nahum on Sunday morning. And he told me nothing about having been shot at.'

'He seems to have wished to keep that secret. What car did Mrs Sulgrave use when she fetched you and drove you home?'

'Her own. It's a small Comet saloon, of last year's make.'

'How did you spend the evening, Miss Rissington?'

'We had dinner, and just as we finished, about half-past eight, some neighbours of Irene's, the Fords, came in. We played bridge until about twelve o'clock.'

'Did either you or Mrs Sulgrave leave High Elms in the course of the evening?'

'Leave the house? No, why should we? Not until I left to come home.'

'Soon after nine o'clock Mr Hardisen saw a small Comet saloon standing at the end of the lane at the bottom of the garden. Could this have been Mrs Sulgrave's car?'

'Not unless somebody took it out of the garage, and

brought it back again. And that doesn't seem altogether likely.'

There seemed to be no object in questioning her any further at the moment. 'Thank you, Miss Rissington,' said Hanslet. 'I need not trouble you any further. But I should like to talk to Mr Hardisen before I go.'

'Then, if you don't mind, I'll leave you to it.' She got up and left the room, the superintendent holding the door open for her.

'Good!' said Hardisen. 'Glad you've finished. Girl was telling the truth. Any fool could see that. What do you want with me?'

'I want you to tell me about your correspondence with Mr Micah Pershore, Mr Hardisen.'

'Not much to tell. We've corresponded for years. Every few months. Queer chap, Micah. Couldn't abide his family. Don't think that queer, though. Cleared out as soon as he could. His mother had left him money. Not much. Just enough to start on. Queer thing was this. Began to want news of his family. Sort of home-sickness. Blood's thicker than water. Wouldn't write to any of them. Wrote to me instead. Asked me to send him news. Used to do it. Told him when his half-sisters died. And their husbands. Now I'll have to write again. Tell him Nahum's gone. Poor old Nahum!'

'When did you last hear from Micah Pershore?'

'Some months back. Can't say when, exactly. Nothing in his letter. Never wrote more than a few words. His letters merely acknowledged mine. Asked after Philip.'

'What did he want to know about Mr Bryant?'

'I'd told him about Philip. Long ago. When he became a lawyer. Micah asked after him in his letter. Wanted to

141

know the name of his firm. And if he was Nahum's man of business. Told him he was. Didn't know about Judson.'

'I gather that Mr Judson was only entrusted with the drawing up of Mr Pershore's will. Mr Bryant acted for his uncle in everything else. Mr Micah Pershore never suggested that he might return to England, I suppose?'

'Not he. Said once he never would. Not while the family lived. Might come back now. When he hears about Nahum. He was the last of them. Second generation don't count. Micah never set eyes on them.'

'You are certain that he is still in the Argentine?'

'Suppose so. Was when I last heard. Said nothing about shifting. His business is there.'

'Well, Mr Hardisen, I'm very grateful to you for having found Miss Rissington for me. I wonder if you'd be good enough to help me a second time?'

'What do you want now?' asked Hardisen suspiciously.

'Just this. I'd like you to cable to Mr Micah Pershore, telling him of his half-brother's death, and let me know what he replies.'

'No harm in that. Good idea. I'll do it for you. What's the notion?'

'I want to be quite sure that he is actually in the Argentine, and not in England.'

Hardisen looked puzzled for a moment, then shook his head. 'I can guess what you're after. Wrong tack, I'm afraid. Micah had nothing to do with it. What would he gain by it? Still, I'll do it. Anything else?'

'What time did you leave Olympia on Monday?'

'About five o'clock. Went from Addison Road to Paddington. Had a drink there. Caught six o'clock to Wells.'

'You didn't by any chance see Mr Bryant at the Motor Show, did you?'

'No, I didn't. Had no idea he was there. Not till Betty said so. Queer thing, that. Philip keeps cropping up. At the Motor Show. In Nahum's study. In his dressing-room, too. No doubt of that.'

'How do you know that he was in his dressing-room?' Hanslet asked.

Hardisen chuckled. 'You might have guessed that. Had a look in the cloak-room? Opposite the study? Can see you haven't. There's no washbasin there. Ought to be. Often told Nahum that. Now you've got it.'

'You mean that if Mr Bryant wanted to wash his hands, he would go up to his uncle's dressing-room?'

'That's it. Nahum always asked men up there. Women were different. Betty saw to them. They've got their own department.'

Hanslet frowned, and then turned suddenly to Hardisen. 'Look here!' he exclaimed. 'You've got it into your head that Mr Bryant knows more about this than he's seen fit to say. Is that just because you dislike him?'

'I don't like him. Told you that long ago. Wouldn't trust him a yard. Not as far as that. That's nothing to do with it. He keeps cropping up.'

'Yes, he keeps cropping up. But he had no earthly motive for desiring his uncle's death, that I can see.'

'Your job to find out. What do you know of Philip? Or his motives? Precious little. I know less. But there's something there. Take my word for that.'

Hanslet was inclined to agree. He arranged with Hardisen that the latter should stay in London for a day or two, or until he had time to cable to Micah Pershore and receive

143

a reply. Then they parted. The superintendent lunched off bread and cheese and a pint of beer, and then proceeded to Byfleet, only a few miles distant.

He inquired for High Elms, and found it to be a fair-sized modern house, in the Willett tradition. He was told that Mrs Sulgrave had come home that morning, and would see him. He was shown into the drawing-room, and Irene Sulgrave appeared.

She was a pretty, vivacious-looking woman, apparently a little older than Betty Rissington, and answered Hanslet's questions without any hesitation. She confirmed Betty's story of the visit to Paris, and the reasons for it having been kept secret. Neither her husband nor Mr Pershore approved of those particular friends of hers. Prejudice, of course. But there was no reason for making trouble if it could be avoided, was there?

Irene Sulgrave also confirmed Betty's account of their doings on Saturday evening. And it seemed almost certain that nobody could have taken out her car without her knowledge. She had locked the garage door, and brought the key into the house with her. There was no sign of the garage door having been forced.

She had not given Mr Pershore a ticket for the Motor Show, and she was quite positive that her husband had not done so. 'As a matter of fact, George and I were talking about Mr Pershore when he was here for the day on Sunday,' she explained. 'George suggested running over there for tea, as we often do. But, you see, Betty had told me that Philip Bryant would be there.'

'Was that any reason why you should not go to Firlands, Mrs Sulgrave?' Hanslet asked.

'No reason at all. But when I told George he would be

there, he gave up the idea. It isn't that he minds Philip. But there was always the risk of Ellen being there.'

'Ellen?' repeated Hanslet. 'Who is she?'

'Philip Bryant's wife. Haven't you met her? I don't want to be catty, but she's the most difficult person in the world to get on with. And she dislikes us as much as we dislike her.'

'I'm surprised at her doing that,' said Hanslet courteously.

Irene Sulgrave smiled. 'That's nice of you,' she replied. 'I don't know what's bitten the woman, but she can hardly speak civilly either to George or to me. And she's very little better with Betty. She's jealous of us, I think. She didn't like Mr Pershore to pay attention to anybody but Philip.'

'Do you know the provisions of Mr Pershore's will, Mrs Sulgrave?'

'No. How should I? I didn't know that he was dead until Betty told me last night, and insisted on leaving for home at once. I rang up George just now, but he was too busy on the stand to tell me anything. So I've really heard nothing. I do hope that Betty inherits his money, and not Philip?'

'Miss Rissington inherits the bulk of the estate. But there is another provision of considerable interest to you, Mrs Sulgrave. You are aware that Mr Pershore held a mortgage upon this house?'

'Yes, I know, and I've been rather worried about what would happen. It was like this. We were in rather low water a few years ago. To tell the truth, we'd had a little flutter, and things went wrong. Betty got out of me what the trouble was, and she must have told her uncle, and asked him to do something about it. He and George's father were great friends, you know.'

'So I have been told,' Hanslet replied.

'Well, Mr Pershore sent for George, and asked him right out how much he wanted to put him on his feet again. George told him that five thousand pounds would do it, and Mr Pershore said that he would tell Philip Bryant to prepare a mortgage on this house for that amount. And he was awfully good about it. He wouldn't accept any interest on it for the first two years, until George's affairs were quite straight again. And I'm sure I don't know how George will find the money to pay back the mortgage, now Mr Pershore is dead.'

'He won't have to, Mrs Sulgrave. Mr Pershore's will provides that the mortgage shall be cancelled, without repayment.'

The superintendent was watching Mrs Sulgrave very closely. There was no mistaking her genuine relief at hearing this. 'Oh, how perfectly sweet of him!' she exclaimed. 'I only wish we had known, and could have thanked him before he died!'

After this, Hanslet had no further questions to ask. Whatever her power of deception might be, he felt convinced that she had had no hand in the attempts upon Mr Pershore's life. He accepted her invitation to a cup of tea, then left High Elms and took a train to Surbiton.

CHAPTER X

The superintendent's visit to Mr Chantley was the outcome of Dr Priestley's suggestion that he should learn all he could of Mr Pershore's past history. He had very little hope of learning anything fresh, but at least he might have the advantage of a different point of view.

He found that Mr Chantley had just returned from his office, and was willing to see him. The man and his surroundings looked exceedingly prosperous. There was an air of good taste about the place which contrasted with the ostentation of Firlands. Mr Chantley, though evidently of a reserved temperament, was quite willing to discuss his relations with Mr Pershore.

'I met him first in the way of business,' he said. 'I had some dealings with the firm in which he was a sleeping partner, and happened to meet him in the office. That was about five years ago, soon after he bought that appalling house at Weybridge. He asked me out to lunch, and an acquaintanceship sprang up. My wife and I went to Weybridge, and he and Miss Rissington came here. In fact, we used to see quite a lot of one another.'

'You became acquainted with Mr Pershore's friends and relations, I suppose?'

'I did,' Chantley replied. He was on the point of adding something to this bald reply, but thought better of it.

Hanslet smiled. He knew the value of unguarded remarks. 'I'd very much like to hear what you were going to say, Mr Chantley,' he said.

'Well, I was going to add, and a rum lot they are. I think I saw you at the funeral yesterday. You may have noticed that the people whom one would most expect to see there were conspicuous by their absence.'

'I noticed that. Miss Rissington, for instance. She was abroad, and had not heard of her uncle's death.'

'Abroad, was she? Did Pershore know of that, I wonder?'

'He did not. Miss Rissington appears to be a lady of independent ideas.'

'Yes, if you like to put it that way. I never could make that girl out. When Pershore was about, butter wouldn't melt in her mouth. As soon as his back was turned she was quite the modern product, with no thought for anybody but herself. My wife began by getting very fond of her, but she received very little encouragement. And yet she was only too ready to give Betty Rissington a good time. Far better than she ever enjoyed in that stuffy place Firlands. However, she seemed to prefer her own rather doubtful friends. That old fellow from Wells, for instance.'

'Mr Hardisen? He had quarrelled with Mr Pershore, I believe?'

'Oh, I don't blame him for that. Pershore was a very difficult man to get on with, unless one was prepared to surrender one's opinions to his. That was the secret of Betty Rissington's success with him. She never contradicted him to his face.'

'She succeeded in becoming the principal beneficiary under his will,' Hanslet remarked.

'Ah! I thought it would turn out that way. The Bryants won't be best pleased. There was a good deal of competition between the cousins. But Bryant was handicapped by not being on the spot. He had a very painstaking ally in his wife, though. But you didn't come here to listen to gossip, Superintendent.'

'To be quite frank, that's just what I did come for, Mr Chantley. No doubt you have read the evidence which was given at the inquest. Had you been a member of the jury, would you have been satisfied that Mr Pershore's death was due to natural causes?'

'I do not think that any layman is qualified to decide upon medical evidence alone,' replied Chantley. 'Especially when that evidence is bewildering, as it certainly was in this case.'

'Well, the police are not satisfied, and I am endeavouring to obtain further information. I cannot do so without an intimate knowledge of Mr Pershore's friends and acquaintances. Listening to what you call gossip is one of my means of gaining this knowledge.'

Mr Chantley's stern expression relaxed in a momentary smile. 'In the hope of thrashing a grain of fact from the chaff of tittle-tattle, I suppose,' he replied. 'I'm not given to gossip, but if I can help you I'm prepared to break my rule. What do you want me to tell you?'

'You mentioned the competition between the cousins,' said Hanslet tentatively.

149

'Oh, that! My wife and I used to get a lot of amusement out of it. On the one side Betty Rissington, and her friend Mrs Sulgrave, of whom Pershore was very fond, by the way. On the other, Bryant and his wife.

'Both sides did their utmost to insinuate themselves. But Bryant wouldn't have stood a chance if it hadn't been for his wife. Bryant always struck me as quite a decent fellow at heart. But he hasn't got a very accommodating manner, and he couldn't always agree with his uncle with the servility which Pershore expected. Mrs Bryant saw this, and set to work to tackle the problem in her own inimitable way.'

Seeing that Chantley paused, the superintendent ventured to urge him on. 'What methods did Mrs Bryant adopt?' he asked.

'Well, I hate discussing these things, especially now that Pershore is dead. But you're a policeman, and our conversation is privileged. Not to put too fine a point upon it, Pershore, like most bachelors of his age, enjoyed the society of good-looking women. Betty Rissington knew what she was about when she asked Irene Sulgrave to her house so often. Mind you, I'm not for a moment suggesting any impropriety. I merely say that he liked to have good-looking women about him. He made no secret of the fact. And he liked them to be safely married. They weren't so likely to set traps for him.

'Now Mrs Bryant is distinctly good-looking and can be extremely charming when she pleases. She set herself the task of ousting Irene Sulgrave, and taking her place in Pershore's affections. I know for a fact, since Pershore told me, that she often came to see him without her husband. And he sometimes took her out to a tête-á-tête lunch in

London. What was the harm? After all, she was his niece-in-law, so to speak.

'If she had been left to herself, her scheme might have succeeded. But she wasn't left to herself. Not by any means. Betty Rissington watched her like a hawk. If she got wind that she was coming to Firlands, she sent for Irene Sulgrave at once. As a counter-irritant, I suppose. And the two of them were positively rude to the unfortunate Mrs Bryant. I've heard them myself, and so has my wife.'

This was interesting, for Hanslet had not hitherto considered Mrs Bryant as a factor in the drama. And it all fitted in with the scraps of information he had already gleaned. 'What is your own personal opinion of Mrs Bryant?' he asked.

'I consider that she is an able and determined woman, with more sense in her head than the other side have between them. I won't say that she has a naturally pleasant nature, but she can be very nice when she wants to be. We have seen nothing of her lately, for the simple reason that she has avoided us. Pershore didn't like his friends to associate with people of whom he disapproved.'

'Surely Mr Pershore cannot have disapproved of you and Mrs Chantley?'

'He could disapprove of anybody who was not prepared to agree with him implicitly upon every point. Don't run away with the idea that I'm trying to paint an unfavourable portrait of him. I'm not. Pershore was a man of many excellent qualities. He made a considerable fortune, entirely by his own efforts. In business matters he was keen, but scrupulously honest. If he said a thing, he meant it, and he never went back upon his word. He could be extremely generous, and he had no real vices. But he had that one fault, an utter intolerance of other people's opinions. If they did not agree with his own, they were contemptible, if not definitely pernicious. And if anybody maintained their own opinions in the face of his displeasure, he never forgave them. He would do his utmost to get his knife into them, or, if that was impossible, he treated them as non-existent.'

'Would it be impertinent of me to ask what terminated the friendship between you and Mr Pershore?' Hanslet asked.

'Not in the least. I ventured to disagree with him, that was all. And the subject of our disagreement was his housekeeper, Mrs Markle.'

The superintendent remembered Mrs Markle's reluctance to discuss the Chantleys. But he said nothing, preferring to await a fuller explanation.

'Mrs Markle's position in the house was a very curious one,' Chantley continued. 'She had all the disadvantages of a menial position without any of the advantages. She was treated like a mere servant, and yet the whole responsibility of the household was hers. On the top of all that, whenever Pershore had a fit of ill-temper, Mrs Markle was always selected to serve as a target.

'I don't think that Pershore deliberately meant to be cruel. But there's no denying that he treated Mrs Markle disgracefully. It was an open secret that they had been brought up together. That fellow Hardisen took care that everybody should know that. He knew them both as children, I believe. And he always made a point of calling Mrs Markle Nancy, which infuriated Pershore, though he couldn't very well object.

'I have never really understood why Pershore treated

Mrs Markle as an inferior being. He knew he was safe enough in doing so. She would never have left him, however he treated her. She was devoted to him, in the sense that a dog is devoted to his master, and Pershore was quite well aware of this. He took advantage of it, in fact. I suppose it pleased him to see the contrast between Mrs Markle's lowly condition and his own prosperity. "Look what I've risen from by my own ability!" You see what I mean?'

'Yes, I see,' replied Hanslet. 'You know perhaps that Mr Pershore provided for Mrs Markle in his will?'

'I didn't know it, but I guessed he had done so. She has earned every penny of it, I can assure you of that. It used to make me writhe to hear the way he spoke to her. And once, a few months ago, I couldn't stand it any longer, and told him what I thought. He replied that he had a perfect right to treat his housekeeper as he pleased. Whereupon I said that no man, however prosperous he might be, had the right to behave like a cad. The result was—well, shall we say a coolness between us. And I'm bound to admit that neither of us took any steps to bridge the gulf.'

'Do you think that Mrs Markle resented the way that Mr Pershore treated her?'

Chantley glanced sharply at the superintendent. 'I don't know,' he replied. 'No doubt you've talked to her. She has always struck me as a woman who kept a tight rein upon her emotions. She never seemed to resent Pershore being rude to her. On the other hand, she never showed any pleasure if he spoke to her pleasantly. I don't fancy that either you or I are capable of discovering what Mrs Markle really feels or thinks. She talks a lot, certainly, but her conversation is all on the surface.'

This was interesting, but the superintendent was at the moment more concerned with the Bryants than with Mrs Markle. 'I understand that the coolness between you and Mr Pershore extended to his nephew and niece, Mr Chantley?' he said.

'To Miss Rissington, certainly. Not so much to Bryant, though I have never seen a lot of him at any time. But we're very good friends when we do happen to meet. As recently as last Monday, for instance.'

'You saw Mr Bryant last Monday?' said Hanslet in some surprise. 'The day of Mr Pershore's death?'

'Yes. Didn't he tell you? I ran into him at the Motor Show. It was about half-past two, or thereabouts. We exchanged a few words, and then separated. I didn't see him again until we met at the funeral yesterday.'

'Was Mrs Bryant with him?'

'No, he was alone. He seemed surprised, almost annoyed, at seeing me there. Just as surprised as I was to hear that Pershore had been there. He and I had at least one thing in common, a lack of interest in motor cars. I have never owned one, and I don't suppose I ever shall. If I have to make a journey by car, I hire. I find it's cheaper and far less trouble.'

'I have not yet discovered the reason for Mr Pershore's visit to Olympia,' said Hanslet.

'Haven't you? Well, perhaps it was the same as mine. Half the people who go to the Derby never see the racing, and half the people who go to the Motor Show don't look at the cars. I certainly didn't. But I'm gregarious by nature. I like a crowd. I like to do what other people are doing. It's a confession of weakness, I dare say.'

'You didn't happen to see Mr Pershore there, I suppose?'

'I did not. We should have been mutually surprised to see one another, I expect. But, a few minutes after my conversation with Bryant, I saw a commotion on one of the stands, and a little later a couple of men going towards it with a stretcher. My curiosity was not sufficient to make me want to see what had happened. In fact, I left the building almost immediately.'

'After Mr Bryant parted from you, did he go towards this stand?'

'It is quite possible. I really couldn't say. I lost sight of him in the crowd.'

'Mr Hardisen was also at Olympia on Monday. Did you happen to see him?'

Mr Chantley shook his head. 'The chances of seeing any particular individual in a crowd like that are very small, you know,' he replied.

After a little further conversation, Hanslet took his leave. The time spent in his visit to Surbiton had not been wasted. Mr Chantley had unconsciously given him a fresh outlook upon the case. And the superintendent felt that he would have to revise his theories in conformity with this outlook. One thing was quite certain. There must be no further delay in interrogating Philip Bryant.

Hanslet returned to London, and took a taxi to the Bryants' flat in Bayswater. He was fortunate in finding Philip at home, and it struck him that there was a certain uneasiness in his welcome. 'This is an unexpected visit, Mr Hanslet,' he said. 'Have you made any fresh discoveries regarding my uncle's death?'

'I am still engaged in collecting facts,' the superintendent replied. 'It is for the purpose of verifying some of these that I have called upon you. In the first place, do you mind telling me where you were at nine o'clock last Saturday evening?'

Philip seemed surprised at this question. 'Where was I?' he replied. 'Yes, I can tell you that. I was at Harrow. A client of mine had asked me to dine with him and discuss a matter of business afterwards.'

'Do you own a car, Mr Bryant?'

'Why, yes. But I didn't drive to Harrow. I went by the Metropolitan from Baker Street, and came back the same way. I reached home shortly before midnight.'

'Did Mrs Bryant accompany you?'

'No. It was a business appointment rather than a social one. She dined early and went to the theatre.'

'What make of car is yours, Mr Bryant?'

'A small Comet saloon. Being a friend of Sulgrave's, I wouldn't dare to buy any other make. Sulgrave is a very good salesman, at least as far as his friends are concerned. He sold me the one I now have last summer. And now he wants me to buy one of their new models.'

'Is that why you went to the Motor Show on Monday afternoon?'

'Partly. But I couldn't get near the Comet stand. That's why I knew nothing of the accident to my uncle. I didn't stay at the Show long. I couldn't afford the time. I was back at my office by four o'clock.'

'Did you meet anybody you know at Olympia?'

'Only a man called Chantley, who used to be a friend of my uncle's. I can't think what he was doing there. Or my uncle either, for that matter. Both of them professed a positive dislike of cars.'

'You didn't happen to see Mr Hardisen at the show, Mr Bryant?'

Philip gave the superintendent a searching glance. 'Hardisen!' he exclaimed. 'No, most certainly I didn't. Was he there?'

'So he informs me. He also says that he saw your uncle, but that they did not speak.'

'Well, that's extraordinary! Hardisen is a queer fellow, with sudden impulses. I've wondered whether he knew anything about this business of my uncle. And now you say that he was at the Motor Show that day. As I told you before, the two of them were at daggers drawn.'

'I have not forgotten that, Mr Bryant. Does Mrs Bryant ever drive your car?'

'Very often. In fact, if we are both out together, she nearly always drives.'

'On Sunday you spent the afternoon at Firlands. After lunch, your uncle took you into the study. Did he leave you alone in the room at any time?'

'Yes, for a minute or two, while he went to the lavatory across the passage.'

'And, of course, you went up to your uncle's dressing-room to wash your hands?'

Hanslet could have sworn that Philip Bryant's eyes shifted at this question. 'Why, yes, of course,' he replied coldly. 'Where else should I go? There's no wash-basin downstairs.'

'Did you by chance go through into Mr Pershore's bedroom while you were upstairs?'

'Into his bedroom!' exclaimed Philip violently. 'Why, whatever put that idea into your head, Mr Hanslet? Why should I do that? I had everything I wanted in the dressing-room.'

'You are quite sure of that, Mr Bryant?' said Hanslet insistently.

'Perfectly certain. The idea of going into the bedroom didn't even occur to me.'

There was a pause, during which Philip fidgeted uncomfortably about the room. And then, suddenly, Hanslet put his next question.

'Do you know the cause of the disagreement between your uncle and Mr Chantley?'

Philip's relief at the change of subject was obvious. 'I don't know for certain,' he replied. 'But I gather that Chantley said something to upset him. My uncle never mentioned the matter to me, but Chantley once hinted that it had something to do with Mrs Markle. It probably began with some trifle, like that ridiculous quarrel with Hardisen. You had a long talk with him after the funeral yesterday, by the way.'

'I had a most instructive conversation with him, Mr Bryant. But we need not discuss that now. You were aware of the clause in Mr Pershore's will, cancelling the mortgage on High Elms. Did you ever mention this to either Mr or Mrs Sulgrave?'

Philip frowned. 'That question amounts to an insult, superintendent,' he replied. 'As a solicitor, I am not in the habit of disclosing my client's confidences.'

'I merely wanted your assurance upon that point. Mrs Markle was no doubt aware that Mr Pershore had made some provision for her?'

'I really can't say, but I should think it extremely probable. Betty knew, and she is almost certain to have given Mrs Markle a hint. You know what women are.'

'You do not think that your uncle is likely to have told Mrs Markle himself?'

'I should think it very unlikely. So far as I know, he

never discussed anything with her beyond ordinary domestic affairs.'

'Isn't that rather curious, considering the intimacy which existed between them, at one time?'

Philip shrugged his shoulders. 'You really can't expect me to criticise the relations which existed between my uncle and his housekeeper,' he replied. 'You'd better talk to Betty. She practically lived in the house, and I didn't. But this I can tell you. Mrs Markle had nothing to complain of. She benefits by my uncle's death, which I most certainly don't. I shall have to put my hand pretty deeply in my pocket to make up the deficiency in the estate.'

'Mrs Markle may have nothing to complain of now,' said Hanslet. 'But don't you think it possible that she resented the way she was treated during your uncle's lifetime?'

A curious expression came into Philip's eyes, as though with the dawning of an entirely new idea. 'It wouldn't have struck me to explore in that direction,' he replied.

'I am bound to explore all directions in search of the truth, Mr Bryant. Whatever may have been the immediate cause of your uncle's death, the inquest on his body showed that previous attempts to murder him had been made. The only alternative is that he had endeavoured unsuccessfully to commit suicide.'

Philip shook his head at this. 'My uncle would have been the last person I should have suspected of anything of the kind,' he replied.

'Then, we are driven to the theory of attempted murder. Now nobody attempts murder without some strong motive for desiring the death of their victim. Who, among your uncle's friends and acquaintances, can we imagine to have had such a motive?'

159

'Well, there are the beneficiaries under the will, to begin with,' Philip replied.

'I have not overlooked them, Mr Bryant. But I feel that other, less obvious motives may have existed. You probably know more about your uncle's affairs than anybody else. Can you offer any suggestions?'

Philip considered this for some time before he replied. 'I didn't know, until you mentioned it just now, that Hardisen was in London on Monday. Have you any idea how long he had been there?'

'Since about midday on Saturday, by his own account.'

'Indeed? As I have already told you, Hardisen and my uncle had quarrelled. From intimate friends they had developed into bitter enemies. And Hardisen is the sort of man who might perform any reckless deed, on the impulse of the moment.'

'I have already formed that opinion,' Hanslet replied, with an inward smile. 'But I find it difficult to understand access to the interior of Firlands prior to your uncle's death. And whoever was responsible for attempting murder certainly had that access.'

Philip frowned, and drummed with his fingers upon the table in front of him. 'You will understand that it is most distasteful to me to discuss these matters,' he said. 'Suspicion must necessarily fall upon my own friends and relations. Has it occurred to you that Hardisen may have had an accomplice already within the house?'

'I have considered that possibility,' Hanslet replied solemnly. 'It has not escaped my notice that Mr Hardisen and Miss Rissington appear to be greatly attached to one another.'

'Betty?' exclaimed Philip. 'That's rather a horrible idea,

isn't it? Perhaps you have also noticed that Hardisen is the only person now living who calls Mrs Markle by her christian name?'

'He knew her when she was a child, I understand.'

'Yes, that is so,' Philip replied deliberately. 'But my uncle didn't like it. And I believe that he had his reasons.'

Hanslet scented mystery in the other's manner. 'What reasons, Mr Bryant?' he asked.

'Oh, reasons that would probably not influence you or me. However my uncle really treated Mrs Markle, he thoroughly appreciated her value to him. He had never been so comfortable before she took over the management of his establishment. And he was desperately jealous of any attempts to lure her away from his service.'

'Had anybody made such an attempt?'

'I don't know. My uncle believed that Hardisen had designs upon her. He mentioned it to me, once, after Hardisen had been staying at Firlands. Hardisen's a widower, you know. My uncle actually suspected him of a desire to marry Mrs Markle. What grounds he may have had for this suspicion I cannot tell you. But I feel pretty certain that it was this idea at the back of his mind which made him ready to quarrel with Hardisen upon such a ridiculous pretext as his letter.'

'Then you consider that if Mr Hardisen had an accomplice in the house, Mrs Markle was the most likely person to fill the rôle?'

'That is my opinion. Mrs Markle's opportunities for attempting to poison my uncle were unlimited. I suspect that Hardisen supplied the means, and that she carried out his scheme.'

Hanslet rose from his seat. 'Well, I'm very much obliged

to you, Mr Bryant,' he said. 'You've given me quite a lot to think about. By the way, do you happen to know the present whereabouts of Mr Micah Pershore, your uncle's half-brother?'

Philip stared at him, and then laughed queerly. 'Micah Pershore,' he exclaimed. 'Why, he's no more than a name to me. He left the country before I was born, so I've always been told. Cut himself off from his family. You can't expect me to know where he is.'

'I thought perhaps you might know,' he replied. 'Well, I needn't waste your time any longer. Good-evening, Mr Bryant.'

He left the flat, and, in spite of the lateness of the hour, took a taxi to Scotland Yard.

CHAPTER XI

The day following Hanslet's conversation with Philip Bryant was Saturday. And on Saturday evenings Doctor Oldland had a standing appointment to dine with Dr Priestley. This particular evening was no exception.

'I had a visit from Button today,' Oldland remarked, as they established themselves in the study after dinner. 'You remember the fellow who carried out the post-mortem on the body of the ill-fated Nahum Pershore. He came to see me in connection with that very matter. Wanted to know if I had any fresh suggestions to offer, in view of the resumption of the inquest next week.'

'Were you able to help him in that respect?' Dr Priestley asked.

'I wasn't, then. Medically speaking, the man's death is a puzzle. All we know is that his heart stopped functioning, for no apparent reason. In the case of death by syncope, the post-mortem reveals the cause. You find some disease of the heart, for instance. Or, at all events, some indication of the heart's failure. In Pershore's case there was nothing of the kind. And whatever effect the discoveries may have had upon his health, neither separately nor together were the indications such as would lead to sudden stoppage of the heart's action.

'Button and I discussed this at length. I needn't trouble you with the details of a highly technical conversation. And, in the end, we were driven to the conclusion that Pershore's death must have been due to what the law calls natural causes. In this case natural is an absurd term. It merely means that no other person was responsible. We decided that the actual cause of death lay in the realms beyond our present knowledge.'

'Not a very satisfactory conclusion,' Dr Priestley remarked.

'A most unsatisfactory one. It worried me, and after Button had gone, I looked up the text-books, to see if I could get any hint there. And, quite by accident, I came across something that I would like to discuss with you. You've got a copy of Dixon Mann, I know.'

He got up and crossed the room to the bookcases with which it was lined. From there he extracted a stout volume, entitled *Forensic Medicine and Toxicology*, by J. Dixon Mann, M.D., F.R.C.P. With this in his hand he returned to his chair.

'I'm going to read you a passage, without comment, if you don't mind,' he said. 'This is it.

'"Death may suddenly result from a blow delivered by a blunt weapon on the pit of the stomach; in such cases it is probable that reflex paralysis of the heart is the cause of death. Maschka records two such cases—in one, a boy was struck with the fist over the stomach; in the other, a strong man was struck over the same region with the flat part of a shovel; both died at once, and in each case the result of the necropsy was negative. Beach records the case of an intoxicated man who was arrested in the street by the police; he resisted so violently that one of the officers struck him a blow with his club in the epigastric region, when he suddenly became quiet and powerless, and on arrival at their destination he was found to be dead; not the least trace of injury could be discovered, neither externally nor internally."'

Oldland laid the book aside. 'As I say, it was only by the merest accident that that passage caught my eye,' he continued. 'But it gave me forcibly to think. The similarity between the cases mentioned and Pershore's death are extraordinary. The sudden collapse and immediate death, for no apparent reason. Dixon Mann says emphatically that the result of the necropsy was negative. That means that the post-mortem revealed nothing which suggested the cause of death. And he goes on to say that in the last case not the least trace of injury, external or internal, could be discovered. And all that forms an exact parallel to our experience in the case of Pershore.'

'That is deeply interesting,' said Dr Priestley. 'It appears to indicate the possibility that Pershore may have died as a result of a blow from a blunt weapon in the pit of the stomach. The possibility from the medical point of view, that is. But surely, in this case, there are certain practical difficulties. I understand that Pershore collapsed in the heart of a dense crowd?'

'Yes, I know. But I don't think that's an insuperable difficulty. The crowd was certainly dense. I had fought my way through it myself, and I know. The book mentions a fist, the flat part of a shovel, and a club. Nothing of the kind could have been used in this case. There simply would not have been room to swing it. But what if in this case the blunt weapon—useful term, that—was exceptionally heavy? Get me?'

Dr Priestley leant back in his chair and fixed his eyes upon the ceiling. 'I understand the trend of your ideas,' he said. 'The intensity of a blow delivered by any object depends upon two factors. These are the weight of that object, and its velocity at the time that the blow is delivered. A light object moving at a high velocity will deliver a blow of the same intensity as a heavy object moving with low velocity.

'In the case of a blow delivered by an object held in the hand, the necessary velocity is obtained by swinging the arm. The objects mentioned in the text-book would require a swing of appreciable length in order to deliver a blow of the requisite intensity. But a very much heavier object, one weighing several pounds, that is, would produce the same result after a swing of only a few inches. Is that your meaning?'

'Exactly. I'll put it this way. A short jab in the tummy from a naked fist is a nasty thing. But I don't think it would be likely to have fatal results. Now, you remember that the Roman gladiators used a thing called a cestus, which was a sort of glove heavily loaded with metal. The idea was to increase the weight of the fist, and so to deliver a more powerful blow with the same length of swing.

'Now the Comet people have decorated their stand at Olympia with lumps of metal of all shapes and sizes. They are, I am told, the component parts of this new transmission of theirs. Suppose that somebody had picked up one of these—they are there for the inquisitive to handle, and some of them are remarkably heavy. A very short jab with such a thing, involving a swing of not more than six inches, would inflict a very severe blow.

'The action might have been intentional, or unintentional. But I can see no practical objection to the theory of this having happened. The crowd was dense, but its very density would have prevented such an action being noticed. They were all standing like tailor's dummies, goggling at the fellow on the stand . . .'

Dr Priestley interrupted him without apology. 'When does the Motor Show end?' he asked.

'Tonight, at ten o'clock,' Oldland replied.

Dr Priestley rose from his chair and glanced at the clock. 'It is now five minutes to nine. We can reach Olympia in twenty minutes in a taxi-cab. I should like to see the actual conditions. Will you accompany me?'

Oldland laughed mirthlessly. He would far rather have sat over the fire, sipping his friend's most excellent whisky. 'I wish I'd kept my mouth shut,' he replied. 'If you insist on dragging me off, there's nothing else for it. All right.'

Harold Merefield was already at the telephone, summoning a taxi. Within five minutes they were on their way, and well before half-past nine they were inside the vast building. As usual the crowd on the last night was overwhelming. Not only the stands, but the passageways between them, seemed to be packed solid with a mass of human beings.

Both Dr Priestley and Oldland were determined men. They had the advantage of a definite object, whereas most of those who surrounded them were wandering without definite purpose. By the exercise of patience and pressure they forced their way to the vicinity of Stand 1001.

Beyond this further progress was impossible. On the

stand itself George Sulgrave, looking utterly fagged out after the strenuous ten days of the Show, was demonstrating the Lovell transmission. His voice was drowned in the deep hum of the crowd. Round him, packed closely together, was a throng of watchers, their eyes fixed upon him as he explained the various points of the chassis before him.

'You see?' Oldland exclaimed. 'Not a man jack of them is taking the slightest notice of his neighbours. Let's see if we can't worm ourselves into the edge of the mob. Then, I think, you'll see for yourself how it could be done.'

It seemed that closing time would come before they accomplished their object. But they insinuated themselves foot by foot towards the stand, until at last they found themselves within a yard or two of it. Here they were hemmed in on every side, and forced to peer over the shoulders of those in front of them if they wished to witness the demonstration. And they were conscious that those behind them were standing on tiptoe, peering over their shoulders in turn.

'We're precisely on the spot where Pershore was standing when he fell,' Oldland whispered. 'I was there, in the front row, actually on the stand itself. Hell!'

His exclamation was caused by a sharp blow under the ribs. He looked quickly about him. Not one of his neighbours had averted his eyes from the demonstration. Dr Priestley, standing beside him was gazing straight in front of him with an expression of rapt attention.

Oldland laughed. 'Example is better than precept,' he said. 'It could be done, you see. You've convinced me, anyhow. And nobody saw you do it. Pershore fell at once, and that scattered the crowd a bit. His assailant took advantage of the confusion to clear off. Now, look down, at the edge of the stand. You see that row of metal parts?'

'Yes, I see them,' said Dr Priestley, after a brief glance. 'They are laid on the woodwork of the stand. But they are joined together by what appears to be stout twine. It would be impossible to raise anyone of them more than a foot or two without disturbing the rest.'

'Hullo, so they are!' Oldland replied. 'That's queer. I'll swear they were lying loose when I was last here. I wonder . . .'

But at that moment the band struck up 'God Save the King.' It was ten o'clock. There was an instant hush, and a pause of immobility as the familiar notes rang out. Then, as the music ceased, the crowd about them dissolved. A slow current of humanity, like the first ebb of the tide, began to sweep towards the exits. The Motor Show was over for that year.

'Well, are you satisfied?' Oldland asked.

'One moment,' Dr Priestley replied. 'I should like to ask a question of one of the attendants on the stand.'

They waited until the current had swept past them. At last there was nobody left between them and the chassis which had been the object of so much curiosity. Dr Priestley stepped forward, and George Sulgrave, who was bustling about in preparation for his own departure, turned and saw him.

'Excuse me,' said Dr Priestley quietly. 'Would you mind telling me why these component parts are tied together in this way?'

Every attendant on a stand at the Motor Show gets used to silly questions. It is his first duty to reply to them with what patience he can command. If he is asked why the tyres are placed on the rim of the wheels, instead of being

169

laid flat upon the roof, he must explain courteously that this is done in order to lessen road shocks. George Sulgrave smiled into the earnest eyes of this elderly gentleman, who had lingered behind in order to propound such a foolish conundrum. 'Why, to prevent anybody making off with them, sir,' he replied.

'I should not have thought that anybody would have been tempted to do such a thing,' Dr Priestley remarked blandly.

'Nor should I. We left them lying loose on the stand, at first. But one of them was actually carried off the other day, and since then we've tied them together, as you see.'

'Was it last Monday that this part was taken?'

George Sulgrave glanced at Dr Priestley in astonishment. 'Yes, it was,' he replied. 'You don't happen to know who took it, do you, sir?'

'I do not. May I ask which particular part it was that was taken?'

Sulgrave pointed to one of the mushroom-shaped pressure valves. 'One of those,' he replied. 'Some idiot picked it up and took it away. He didn't carry it far. Found it too heavy, I expect. He put it in one of the cars on the Solent stand. A friend of mine there found it and brought it back in the evening.'

Dr Priestley surveyed the pressure valve with interest. 'Can you tell me the weight of this piece of metal?' he asked.

But Sulgrave was getting impatient. 'About twelve pounds, I believe. But may I remind you sir, that the Show is closed. If you wish for further particulars, and would care to call at our showrooms on Monday, I should be happy to give you any information you may require.'

But Dr Priestley's curiosity was satisfied. Having bidden Sulgrave a polite good-night, he and Oldland made their way to the exit which they reached as the last stragglers were leaving. Dr Priestley noticed that almost the last stand they passed was that of the Solent Motor Car company.

They took a taxi back to Westbourne Terrace, and there, in the study, they found Merefield entertaining Superintendent Hanslet. 'Hullo, Professor!' exclaimed the latter as they entered the room. 'I thought you wouldn't mind me waiting. I turned up about half an hour ago, and Mr Merefield told me that you had gone to the Motor Show. You left it a bit late, didn't you?'

Dr Priestley seemed to be in an excellent humour. 'Better late than never, superintendent,' he replied cheerfully. 'A most interesting experience. Most interesting indeed. Have you come to tell me that you have solved the mystery of Mr Pershore's death?'

'I'm not far off the solution, I fancy. But before I tell you my news, I think that Mr Merefield has something to say.'

'I've had another visitor, sir,' said Harold. 'He came about a quarter of an hour before the superintendent, and asked for him. He said that he had been told at Scotland Yard that he would find him here. He wouldn't wait, and he wouldn't give his name, but he said that he would come back later. He seemed very anxious to see Mr Hanslet as soon as possible.'

'So I waited here, in order not to miss him,' said Hanslet. 'He hasn't turned up again yet, I rather fancy, from Mr Merefield's description, that he is my friend Hardisen.'

'I should be very pleased to make his acquaintance,' replied Dr Priestley. 'Meanwhile, I am anxious to learn how nearly you have approached to the solution of the mystery.'

Hanslet repeated his conversations with Betty Rissington, Mrs Sulgrave, Mr Chantley and Philip Bryant. 'I'm beginning to understand the conditions which existed before Pershore's death,' he continued. 'He seems to have been surrounded by people, all anxious to make away with him, but for different reasons. And these people seem to group themselves into pairs.

'First of all, we have Miss Rissington and her friend Mrs Sulgrave. They both protest that they knew nothing whatever about the affair. Miss Rissington had the necessary opportunities. Both of them benefit under Pershore's will. And they had a representative at Olympia at the time of his death, in the shape of Mrs Sulgrave's husband.

'Then we have Hardisen and Mrs Markle. Hardisen admits having shot at Pershore on the preceding Saturday evening. Mrs Markle's opportunities were even better than Miss Rissington's. Hardisen quite freely told me that he wanted to get his own back upon Pershore. Mrs Markle may well have resented her treatment at Firlands. Hardisen confesses to having been at Olympia at the time of Pershore's death.

'Lastly, Mr and Mrs Bryant. Bryant's manner, when I first saw him on Monday evening, was queer. His opportunities existed, though they were not so good as those of the other two groups. His motive is not yet revealed, though I believe that I have an inkling of it. He was seen by Mr Chantley at the Motor Show. But he made no mention of his presence at the Motor Show until I taxed him with it.'

'And which, if any, of these groups do you consider to be guilty?' Dr Priestley asked.

'That's just what I came here to talk to you about, Professor. I look at it this way. One of these groups made two attempts to murder Pershore, by means of the olives and the inhalant. I don't count the shooting, for that may have been merely a passing impulse of Hardisen's. Since these attempts failed, they had another shot, and succeeded. But how they can have done him in at the Motor Show, I'm blest if I know.'

'There we may be able to help you,' said Dr Priestley. 'Since it involves medical details, perhaps you will be good enough to explain our suspicions to the superintendent, Oldland?'

Oldland picked up the text-book, and once more read the significant passage. 'We went straight to Olympia, where Priestley made the necessary experiment, with myself as the victim. I can feel the effects now, and shall prescribe a drop of whisky for myself.'

He poured himself out a glass, and sipped it appreciatively. 'That's better,' he said. 'Now Priestley, in that insinuating way of his, discovered that a heavy lump of metal had been removed from the Comet stand some time on Monday. What did the fellow call it? A pressure valve, that's it. It's a mushroom-shaped piece of steel, weighing twelve pounds. Just the thing for the job. You hold it by the stem, and punch the other fellow in the tummy with the head. A perfect blunt weapon, as the book calls it. The head must be fully six inches across, and wouldn't leave the vestige of a mark.'

'The method of the crime is, I think, apparent,' Dr Priestley remarked. 'Mr Pershore's assailant contrived to get next to him in the crowd round Stand 1001. Mr Pershore may or may not have noticed his presence. He picked up the pressure valve, and with it delivered a short sharp blow, similar to the blow I struck Oldland with my fist. Mr Pershore fell instantly, and his assailant made off, hiding the pressure valve under his coat.'

'And disposed of it on the first opportunity,' Oldland continued. 'He was making for the exit, and came to the Solent stand. You know what people do at the Motor Show. They walk on to a stand, look round, and get into one of the cars. They pretend that their object is to find out if the seats are comfortable, but it isn't. They merely want a rest. The attendants on the stand are used to this sort of thing, and they don't take much notice. This fellow went and sat in one of the Solent cars, dumped his blunt weapon there, and then walked out. Easy as shelling peas.'

'Well, I'm immensely obliged for the explanation,' said Hanslet. 'That's another bit of the jig-saw put in its place. Now, how does it help us to find the criminal? Sulgrave appears to be cut out, since he was actually demonstrating at the time. Hardisen and Bryant remain as possibles. It sounds just the sort of trick that Hardisen might have played. I'm quite sure that in the mood he was then he would thoroughly have enjoyed punching Pershore in the stomach. But, on the whole, I'm inclined to plump for Bryant, in spite of the fact that his motive is obscure.'

'What motives have you for suspecting Mr Bryant?' Dr Priestley asked.

'Several. In the first place there is Mrs Bryant. She was doing her best to cut out Miss Rissington. Her idea was to curry favour with Pershore, in the hope of inducing him to alter his will to her husband's advantage. And I haven't a doubt that she was the woman in the garden at Firlands on Saturday evening.

'I told you what Bryant said to me yesterday evening. Since then, I've been making inquiries. It's quite true that he has a small Comet saloon car, which he keeps in a mews not far from his flat. And it is quite true that on Saturday night he was dining with a client in Harrow. He did not leave his friend's house until close upon eleven o'clock. On the other hand, Mrs Bryant was seen to take the car from the mews shortly before eight. I haven't yet found anybody who saw her return.

'Now Weybridge is only eighteen miles from London. She could have reached Firlands comfortably in three-quarters of an hour. And there's another point. When I questioned Mrs Markle about the telephone call for Pershore that evening, she suggested that the voice might have been Mrs Bryant's.

'If it was Mrs Bryant, what was her game? I've got a theory which will explain that. She heard by chance that Miss Rissington would be out that evening, and she saw the opportunity of having a private interview with Pershore. I think that she entered the garden by the door on to the lane, having sent Pershore a message to expect her.

'What passed between them, I have no idea. Nor am I sure whether her husband knew of her exploit or not. But I have to bear in mind the possibility that this was the occasion on which the poisoned olives were introduced into the cupboard. As I have explained, it is possible to reach the study from the garden without passing through any other part of the house.'

Hanslet paused, and glanced inquiringly at Dr Priestley. But the latter merely nodded impatiently. 'You have other grounds of suspicion against the Bryants, I gather?' he asked.

175

'Certainly, Professor,' Hanslet replied. 'I'll set them out in order for you. First of all, when he was at Firlands on Sunday, he declared that he smelt an escape of gas, which nobody else was able to detect. His idea was to create a false impression. If he knew that his uncle was about to die, and that the post-mortem would reveal the presence of carbon monoxide, his evidence would suggest the source of the poison. There would be no need to search further, and the faked inhalant would escape discovery. A further point in connection with this is the fact that, immediately I told him that there was a case of poisoning in the house, he asked if it was due to gas.

'Then, when I questioned him yesterday evening, his answers were perfectly calm and collected until I suggested that he had gone up to Pershore's dressing-room to wash his hands. He was on the defensive at once. In fact, he got very near the blustering stage. And his denial that he had been in the bedroom was quite unnecessarily forcible. Curiously enough, when I tackled him about being down in the study, he was quite calm. I came to the conclusion that while he knew something about the inhalant, he had had no hand in the olives. That's why I think that Mrs Bryant had already put them in the cupboard on the previous evening.

'There's just one more point. You remember that the faked inhalant contained zinc filings. This morning I called on Bryant at his office, to see if I could get anything more out of him. I got nothing definite. But one thing I did notice. The outside sill of the window of his room is covered with sheet zinc. A narrow strip of this has recently been cut off. When I drew Bryant's attention to this, he grew very confused, but he declared that he had no

176

knowledge how it happened, and that he had never noticed it before.'

Again the superintendent paused, hoping for some comment from Dr Priestley. But it was Oldland who spoke. 'You seem to have got a pretty good case against the Bryants,' he said. 'But there are two things one would like to know. First of all the motive, of which you say you have an inkling. And then, assuming Bryant to have been the wielder of the pressure valve, how did he know that his uncle intended to visit the Motor Show?'

'I'd rather not talk about the motive until I have further information,' Hanslet replied. 'Miss Rissington, in her conversation with me, suggested the answer to the second point. She said that her uncle might have made an appointment to meet Bryant at the Motor Show, in order to discuss something of a confidential nature. I've been wondering if it had anything to do with Mrs Bryant's visit to Firlands on Saturday evening, and its sequel.'

'Sounds a bit thin to me,' said Oldland doubtfully. 'Hullo! that sounds like the return of Harold's mysterious visitor.'

There was certainly a sound of voices in the hall. Merefield went out, to find Mr Hardisen in conversation with the parlourmaid. 'Will you come in here?' he said. 'Mr Hanslet is here now.'

The new arrival followed Harold into the study. Hanslet rose to greet him. 'Good-evening, Mr Hardisen,' he said. 'You want to see me, I understand. Let me introduce you to my friends. Dr Priestley, Doctor Oldland, Mr Merefield.'

'Evening, gentlemen,' replied Hardisen. 'Nice and snug here. Better than the Yard. Dug yourself in, eh, superintendent? Been chasing you all the evening. Off and on.

Got something to show you. Answer to my cable. Thought you'd like to see it.'

He thrust a piece of paper into the superintendent's hand. It was a cable from the Argentine, addressed to Hardisen at his London hotel, and ran as follows: 'Micah Pershore died fourth instant Capes Bryant and Capes solicitors informed by cable.'

Hanslet read it aloud. 'What do you make of this, Mr Hardisen?' he asked.

Hardisen made a gesture suggestive of the tying of a noose round his neck. Then he grinned maliciously. 'Good enough to hang Philip,' he replied.

CHAPTER XII

'Won't you sit down, Mr Hardisen?' said Dr Priestley courteously. 'And perhaps you will allow me to offer you some refreshment. You will find whisky on that table.'

'I'll sit down,' Hardisen replied. 'Glad to. But not whisky, thank you. Not in the evening. No body to it. Only one thing to drink after dinner. Vintage port.'

Dr Priestley nodded to Harold, who slipped out of the room. Hanslet took the opportunity of drawing his chair up to Hardisen's. 'I don't understand you, Mr Hardisen,' he said. 'You can talk quite freely here. These gentlemen know the outlines of the Pershore case. How is this cable evidence against Mr Bryant?'

Hardisen glanced at him witheringly. 'Ever asked Philip about Micah?' he said.

'I did so yesterday, and he told me that he knew nothing whatever about him.'

'Then he's a liar. Look at the paper. Plain as a pikestaff. Micah dead. Dies last Thursday week. Cable to Capes Bryant and Capes. That's Philip's firm. Eh?'

'Why do you suppose Mr Bryant denied all knowledge of Mr Micah, then?'

'Why? Any fool could see that. Philip is Nahum's residuary legatee. Know what that means?'

'I don't see what that has to do with Mr Micah Pershore's death, Mr Hardisen.'

'You don't? Listen to me. Micah wasn't a young man. Had a hard life. Before he made his pile, that is. Never told me he was ill. Might have been, for all that. Queer, that last letter of his. Asking about Philip. Whether he acted for Nahum. Couldn't make it out. See it all now, though.'

At this moment Harold returned, bearing a bottle in a wicker cradle and a wine glass. Mr Hardisen watched him anxiously. 'Careful, my boy!' he exclaimed. 'Don't disturb it. Can't be too careful. Not with old port. Ruin it in a moment. Ah!'

He took the glass which Harold handed to him, and sipped it with the air of a connoisseur. 'First-class wine,' he murmured. 'Congratulate you, Dr Priestley. On your wine merchant. Knows his job. Like to meet him. I'm a wine merchant myself.'

'I have no doubt that could be arranged, Mr Hardisen,' Doctor Priestley replied. 'You were speaking of Mr Micah Pershore's last letter to you?'

'That's right. Why did he want to know about Philip? Not for Philip's sake. He knew all about him. I'd told him. Conceited ass. Too big for his boots. Not like his cousin Betty. She's a good girl.'

Mr Hardisen sipped his port approvingly. But Hanslet had no patience with these dilatory methods. 'Why did Mr Micah want to know whether Mr Bryant was Mr Nahum's solicitor?' he asked.

'Ought to guess that. I can. Remember what I said? Blood's thicker than water. Micah feels the end coming. What about his money? Who's to have that? Thinks of his family. Half-brother still alive. Nearest relation. Makes a will in Nahum's favour. Says nothing about it. Too proud for that. Doesn't want any communication. Not while he's alive. No last minute reconciliation. Micah wasn't that sort. Instructs his man. Out in the Argentine. Cable Bryant when he dies. Tell him about the will. Got it now?'

Dr Priestley anticipated Hanslet's reply. 'Fill up Mr Hardisen's glass, Harold,' he said. 'You think that Mr Bryant knew, before last Monday, of Mr Micah Pershore's death, and that he had made a will in Mr Nahum Pershore's favour?'

'Sure of it,' Mr Hardisen replied confidently. 'Explains a lot of things.'

'The position then, would be this. Since Mr Micah died on the fourth, Mr Nahum, at the time of his death on the eighth, had already inherited his money. Mr Nahum's estate will thus be increased by the amount of Mr Micah's bequest to him.'

'You've got it,' Mr Hardisen replied. 'That's where Philip comes in. Couldn't make out that offer of his. Make up the deficiency. Why should he? Not for love. Too mean for that.'

'Mr Bryant's actual position is this. If the yield of his uncle's estate was as expected, he, as the residuary legatee, had little prospect of benefit. But if that estate is increased by Mr Micah's bequest, he will benefit by probably the whole amount of that bequest.'

Hardisen nodded. 'That's right. See Philip's game? He knew of Micah's death. And of his will. Kept it dark. For this reason. As soon as Nahum heard, what then? I know. He'd have altered his own will. Increased Betty's legacy. Didn't mean Philip to get the lion's share. Not he.'

By this time Hanslet had got a grasp of the situation. 'By Jove, there's Bryant's motive!' he exclaimed. 'He had to kill his uncle before he learnt the terms of Micah's will. He was the one who stood to gain the most, all along, though nobody knew it.'

'What did I tell you?' Mr Hardisen murmured. 'Keep your eye on Philip. That's what I said. First time we met. Didn't I now?'

'You did, Mr Hardisen. Do you think that Mrs Bryant was in the secret?'

'Ellen? Damned if I know. Shouldn't think so. Philip's too close for that. Wouldn't trust a woman. Not even his wife. Why?'

'Because I have reason to believe that the woman who came out of the Firlands' garden last Saturday evening was Mrs Bryant.'

Hardisen shrugged his shoulders. 'Shouldn't wonder. Might have been her. Always making up to Nahum. Betty told me. Wanted to get her finger in the pie. Not the first time she's met him like that, I dare say. On the quiet. Through the garden. Into the study. Snug little tête-à-têtes. Betty guessed something was up. Didn't know it was Ellen though.'

'I should be interested to know what Miss Rissington guessed,' said Hanslet eagerly.

'Servants' gossip. Told me about it. When she was at Wells. Happened just before then. Parlourmaid found it. One that was poisoned. What's the girl's name? Jessie, that's right.'

'What did Jessie find, Mr Hardisen?'

'Coming to that. Thought it was Miss Betty's, naturally. Showed it to her. Betty said it wasn't hers. Where did it come from? Jessie told her. In Nahum's study. When she was dusting that morning. Behind a chair. Woman's handkerchief. Lace-edged and all.'

'Did Miss Rissington know the owner of the handkerchief?'

'Not she. Wasn't hers, that's all. Asked Nancy Markle. She didn't know. Couldn't understand it. No woman been in there. Not that would use a handkerchief like that. Not so far as she knew.'

'I suppose nobody thought of asking Mr Pershore if he could account for the handkerchief?'

'Not likely! Who would have asked him? Betty? Nancy Markle? He'd have jumped down their throats. Asked them how he was to know. They'd let some woman into the room. While he was out. I can just hear him.'

'And what is your own opinion about this handkerchief, Mr Hardisen?' Dr Priestley asked.

Hardisen glanced at him and winked vulgarly. 'One of Nahum's little games. Fond of women. Just how fond I can't say. How did he spend his time? Not at his office. Went to see his friends. Didn't know he encouraged them at Firlands, though. Not till I saw that woman the other night. Getting late. Time I went home to bed.'

He finished his glass of port and refused Dr Priestley's invitation to another. Harold rang for a taxi for him, and saw him off the premises.

'Well, superintendent, what about it now?' asked Oldland, who had been an interested listener to the conversation.

'It's a perfectly clear case against Bryant,' Hanslet replied.

'Whatever may have been the reason for Mrs Bryant's secret visits to Pershore, it's her husband who took the final step. I suspected him all along, and now we've got his motive all cut and dried.'

'Hardly that,' Dr Priestley objected. 'So far it is only a matter of conjecture that Mr Micah made a will in his half-brother's favour, and that Mr Bryant knew this.'

'I'll soon find that out, Professor,' Hanslet replied. 'I'm going to have another interview with him, first thing in the morning. And I shall have a warrant for his arrest in my pocket.'

'What will you charge him with?' Oldland asked. 'You've got no definite proof that he punched his uncle in the tummy.'

'I shall charge him with attempted murder, by means of the faked inhalant. That will do to be getting on with. The actual murder charge can follow later. And now I think I'll follow Hardisen's example and get off to bed.'

Thus only Oldland remained of Dr Priestley's visitors. 'Well, what do you really think of it all?' he asked.

Dr Priestley took off his glasses, wiped them deliberately, and replaced them. 'I think that the superintendent is acting with undue precipitation,' he replied.

'Do you? It seems to me that Bryant is undoubtedly the man.'

'Very possibly,' Dr Priestley replied. 'On the other hand, the innocence of the other persons involved has not been established. And I am by no means certain that the real motive of the crime, if indeed a crime has been committed, has yet been discovered.'

Hanslet was as good as his word. The next day being Sunday, he felt pretty certain of finding Philip at home. He called at the flat at ten o'clock in the morning, and demanded an interview.

Philip was obviously displeased at his visit. 'Well, super-intendent, what is it now?' he asked curtly.

'I've got a cable from the Argentine that I should like to read to you, Mr Bryant,' Hanslet replied. 'It refers me to your firm for certain information.'

Philip grew suddenly white. 'A cable from the Argentine!' he exclaimed. 'I don't understand you. We have no dealings with anybody in the Argentine.'

Hanslet took the cable from his pocket, and, without mentioning the address, read it out slowly. 'I'd like your comment upon that, Mr Bryant,' he said.

For a few seconds Philip made no reply. Hanslet, watching him, saw that he had received a severe blow, and that he was striving desperately to recover from it. 'Who sent you that cable?' he asked at last, in a harsh strained voice.

'It was not sent to me, but to Mr Hardisen. Perhaps you didn't know that he has been for many years in correspond-ence with Mr Micah Pershore?'

'Hardisen!' exclaimed Philip, in a tone of utter amaze-ment. 'Good Lord, I never thought . . .' He checked himself, and laughed weakly. 'He's been pulling your leg, superin-tendent. You can't believe a word a chap like that says. Why, you know very well that he and my uncle had become bitter enemies. I've had my suspicions, all along, that he had something to do with my uncle's death. This cable is part of his game. Can't you see that?'

Hanslet shook his head reprovingly. 'Now, you're a sensible man, Mr Bryant,' he said. 'You must realise that it is no good trying to play with me. You know as well as

I do that you need not answer my questions. And you also know that it can do you no possible good to answer them falsely. I ask you when you received information of the death of Mr Micah Pershore?'

'I know nothing whatever about Micah Pershore, alive or dead,' Philip replied angrily. 'I told you that a couple of days ago, if I remember rightly.'

'You did, I am sorry to say, Mr Bryant. But, unfortunately, I have evidence that that statement was false. I have been to the office of the cable company and searched their files. Among the copies of messages received was one from a firm of lawyers in Buenos Aires, addressed to Capes Bryant and Capes, Lincoln's Inn Fields, London. This cable was despatched on the fifth of this month. The wording is as follows, "Micah Pershore died yesterday stop Nahum Pershore of Firlands Weybridge sole legatee stop confirmation follows next mail." Now, Mr Bryant, do you still persist in your statement?'

Philip's face turned a sickly yellow. But he made a final effort to defend himself. 'A cable from an unknown source has no legal authority,' he replied. 'I am bound to await confirmation before I can place any reliance upon the information it contained.'

'That is beside the point. You will admit that you received this cable?'

'What if I did? I cannot see that it is any business of yours.'

'My business is to investigate the attempts made upon your uncle's life, Mr Bryant. In the course of that investigation, I am bound to consider the question of motive. Your knowledge of Mr Micah's death, and of the provisions of his will, supplies a very potent motive for you to desire your uncle's death.'

'I don't know what you're talking about!' Philip exclaimed. 'That's sheer nonsense. Where's the motive?'

'Come now, Mr Bryant,' replied Hanslet impatiently. 'Let me ask you once more to be reasonable, and not to waste the time of both of us like this. If your uncle died before he had time to alter his will, you, as his residuary legatee, would inherit the bulk of Mr Micah's fortune.'

'That's preposterous! Why should my uncle have altered his will?'

'That you should know better than I. You, evidently, were not prepared to risk it. Your preparation of a mixture of zinc filings and chalk, and your substitution of this mixture for your uncle's inhalant, sufficiently proves that.'

Hanslet spoke accusingly, and this second blow told. It was obvious to the superintendent that Philip had hoped all along that the faked inhalant had not been discovered. Faced with this knowledge, so convincingly expressed, his resistance broke down completely. He slumped forward in his chair, and covered his face with his hands.

But Hanslet, as was his duty, pursued his advantage relentlessly. 'You substituted your mixture for the inhalant some time during last Sunday,' he said. 'The necessary evidence of your having done so is in my possession. But, in your own interests, I suggest to you that it may be to your ultimate advantage to make a full statement.'

Philip raised his head and stared dully at the superintendent. 'What do you want to know?' he asked.

'I won't trouble you to give details of the inhalant dodge. I know all about that already. But that was not the only attempt you made upon your uncle's life. You prepared a bottle of poisoned olives, and you placed, or caused someone else to place, these olives in the cupboard in your uncle's study.'

Philip shook his head feebly. 'I confess to the faked inhalant,' he replied. 'I was a fool not to take greater precautions than I did. But I swear by everything I hold sacred that I know nothing whatever about the olives.'

'Then you place me under the painful necessity of charging Mrs Bryant with that crime,' said Hanslet sternly.

'Ellen! She knows nothing of it. I have never breathed a word to her about it. Besides, how could she have put the olives in the cupboard? She never went to Firlands for at least a fortnight before my uncle's death.'

'That is hardly correct. You must be aware that Mrs Bryant visited your uncle in the evening of last Saturday week. And you will hardly deny that she was in the habit of visiting him secretly?'

'I do deny it, most positively. What could have been the object of those visits?'

'Their ultimate object was persuasion. You and Mrs Bryant wished to influence your uncle to alter his will in favour of one or both of you.'

'Damn you!' exclaimed Philip fiercely. 'Ellen was jealous of Betty and allowed herself to let it be seen. I know that. But to say that she had secret interviews with my uncle is merely ridiculous. He wasn't fond enough of her to allow that.'

Hanslet shrugged his shoulders incredulously. 'Can you prove that Mrs Bryant was not at Firlands, having driven there in her car, at nine o'clock on the evening of the thirteenth?'

A momentary gleam of triumph came into Philip's eyes. 'You could have proved it for yourself, superintendent,' he replied. 'She has been served with a summons for leaving her car unattended outside a theatre in Chiswick, from eight o'clock until eleven that evening. You can see the summons for yourself, if you like. And your position will enable you to elicit the facts from the policeman who took the particulars.'

This was a check, but not, Hanslet assured himself, a very serious one. 'Mrs Bryant's presence at Firlands that evening is not essential to the matter,' he said. 'I have reason to believe that the olives were put in the cupboard at an earlier date than that. You have admitted that you placed the faked inhalant in your uncle's bedroom. You will not ask me to believe that some other agent, entirely unknown to you, made an independent attempt upon your uncle's life by means of the poisoned olives?'

'I ask you to believe nothing, superintendent,' Philip replied, rather more calmly. 'You have accused me of attempting to murder my uncle. I confess to having tampered with the Hewart's Inhalant in his bedroom at Firlands, some time between one and half-past last Sunday afternoon. Since the effects of the false inhalant in no way contributed to my uncle's death, you cannot bring a very serious charge against me. And I most emphatically deny that either I or my wife have any knowledge whatever of any other design upon my uncle's health or comfort.'

'Well, we won't press the point of the poisoned olives,'

said Hanslet. 'No doubt my inquiries will enable me to trace the agency by which they were placed in the cupboard in your uncle's study. You told me that you owned a Comet car, did you not?'

'Yes, in common with a good many other people. It's a popular make, you know.'

'As the owner of a Comet car, your principal interest at the Motor Show would naturally be the Comet Stand?'

'Well, I don't know about that. I went to Olympia to see several things that interested me.'

'Among them, no doubt, was the new transmission shown on the Comet Stand?'

'George Sulgrave told me, before the show opened, that his firm had something sensational up their sleeve. When I went to Olympia on Monday, I intended visiting the Comet stand, but the crowd was so great that I could not get near it without waiting for a considerable time. And this I was not prepared to do. I knew that I had only to wait until the show was over to see the demonstration chassis in the London showrooms. I could then have had it explained to me in comfort.'

'Have you ever thought of buying a Solent car?'

'George Sulgrave will take very good care that I buy nothing but a Comet, so long as he is employed by that firm. In any case, I don't think I'm particularly drawn towards the Solent.'

'You did not visit the Solent stand on Monday?'

'No, I certainly did not.'

'Did you know that your uncle was at Olympia on Monday?'

'I did not. I cannot understand what induced him to go there. On the previous day, while I was at Firlands, I mentioned that I should look in at the show on Monday afternoon if I had time. My uncle made no suggestion that he intended to be there at the same time.'

Hanslet nodded. 'Then you didn't see him when you visited the Comet stand?' he asked conversationally.

'I did not see my uncle at Olympia,' Philip replied firmly. 'Nor did I visit the Comet stand. I was not able to approach it within several yards.'

'That's a pity. There are several things about the new transmission which would have interested you. One of its essential parts is the pressure valve. But I dare say that your friend Mr Sulgrave has told you all about it?'

Philip shook his head. 'I know nothing about it,' he replied. 'I haven't seen George since the show opened, and before that he was pledged to secrecy.'

'This pressure valve is a mushroom-shaped piece of steel. It weighs about twelve pounds and is very convenient to hold. Just the thing to hit anybody with, in fact.'

But Philip's expression showed no trace of confusion. 'I really haven't the slightest idea why you should imagine that this pressure valve should have any interest for me,' he replied. 'I do not claim to possess a mechanical mind. So long as a car gives me satisfaction, I do not trouble myself about the details of its construction.'

'I see. You can't offer any explanation of your uncle's remarkably sudden death at Olympia?'

'I have no explanation to offer. In my own defence, I could point out that the medical evidence is to the effect that it was in no way due to the effects of carbon monoxide poisoning. That, in itself, proves my innocence.'

Hanslet had made up his mind as to his procedure. He had delivered his blow, and had forced Philip into a partial

191

confession. He had hoped, by following up his advantage, to make this confession complete. Since he had failed, he would adopt other tactics.

'I came here this morning provided with a warrant for your arrest, Mr Bryant,' he said. 'I shall not, however, execute that warrant. What further action I may take in consequence of the statement which you have made I cannot at present say. I should recommend you to consider very seriously your position. The sudden death of your uncle, following immediately upon your attempt to poison him with carbon monoxide, will, no doubt, be considered as significant by the coroner's jury. Good-morning.'

And, without giving Philip time to reply, he left the flat and took a taxi to Scotland Yard.

There he sent for Inspector Jarrold, and informed him of the latest developments of the case. 'Bryant's our man,' he said. 'We've got his motive, and we know now how he did it. We could proceed against him on a charge of attempted murder. But I don't think we've got enough evidence yet to convince a jury on the capital charge. I'm inclined to give him rope, and perhaps he will hang himself.'

'Meaning that you won't arrest him just yet?'

'That's it. I want you to have both him and Mrs Bryant shadowed. One or other of them may give themselves away. Or Bryant may try to make a bolt for it, and that would be additional proof of his guilt. Meanwhile, I'm going to try to find out if anyone else saw him at Olympia on Monday. And I'm going to start with Sulgrave.'

That same afternoon saw Hanslet at High Elms. He asked for an interview with George Sulgrave, which was readily accorded him. But George, though anxious to be helpful, could not tell him very much.

'I was demonstrating on the stand nearly twelve hours a day,' he said. 'From morning till night there was a surging crowd round it. But you can understand that I could only see and recognise people in the front row, and then I had no time to speak to them personally. I never saw Mr Pershore at all. I did not know until next day who it was that had fainted by the stand. And I certainly never saw Philip Bryant, though he had promised to visit the stand if he could manage it.'

'Were you surprised when you heard that Mr Pershore had visited the Motor Show?'

George Sulgrave smiled. 'I certainly expressed surprise,' he replied. 'But I wasn't really so astonished as I pretended to be.'

'Had you asked him to visit the Comet stand, then?' Hanselet asked suspiciously.

'Oh, no, I should never have thought of doing that. Pershore always professed a dislike of cars and everything connected with them. But, as a matter of fact, he was one of our customers.'

'One of your customers!' Hanslet exclaimed. 'Do you mean that he intended to buy a car from you?'

'More than that. He actually bought a car from us, last June.'

This seemed so much at variance with all that Hanslet had hitherto heard that he stared at Sulgrave incredulously. 'Are you quite sure of that?' he asked.

'Perfectly certain. He asked me to keep it a dead secret, and up till now I have done so. Now that he's dead, I suppose there's no harm in telling the whole story, if you want to hear it.'

'I do most decidedly want to hear it,' Hanslet replied.

'Well, one day last June, Pershore rang me up at the showrooms. He said he was alone, since Betty was away for a few days, and asked me if I would dine with him one night. We fixed up a date and I went.

'After dinner he took me into that study of his, and said he wanted to talk business. He was such a long time coming to the point, that at first I couldn't make out what he wanted. He talked about Betty. How fond he was of her, and how he liked to give her everything she wanted. Finally he said that he'd made up his mind to give her a surprise. He was going to buy her a car and give it her on her birthday.'

'When is Miss Rissington's birthday?' Hanslet asked.

'Some time in August. But, so far as I know, she never got the car. Or, if she did, she never said anything to me about it. Pershore impressed upon me that it was to be a great secret, and made me promise faithfully that I would never breathe a word to anybody. He went so far as to hint that if anything came out about this car, he would make things unpleasant for me. He was referring to the mortgage on this house, of course.'

'One moment, Mr Sulgrave. Did you know that he intended that the mortgage should be cancelled on his death?'

'I did not. More than once he had hinted that he intended to do something for me, for my father's sake. But I had no idea what he meant to do. I certainly didn't expect what amounts, in effect, to a legacy of five thousand pounds.'

Hanslet was impressed by the sincerity of his tone. 'All right, go ahead,' he said. 'I'm sorry I interrupted you.'

'I gave the required promise, and asked him what type of car he wanted. He replied that he knew nothing about cars, which was quite true. It was essential that the car he bought should be exactly like Philip Bryant's, down to the smallest detail. Same horse-power, same type of body, same colour. I told him that since Philip's car was standard in every way, there would be no difficulty about that.

'He asked me when the car would be ready for him, and I replied that he could have delivery a week from that day. I explained the formalities of registration and insurance, and told him that I could do all that for him. He gave me a cheque for the whole amount then and there, and I carried the deal through.'

'But what became of the car?' Hanslet demanded.

'I haven't the slightest idea where it is now. Pershore told me that when the car was ready, he would send a man to collect it, and that he would meanwhile arrange for somewhere for it to be kept till Betty's birthday. The man duly turned up, armed with Pershore's authorisation, and that's the last I heard of it. Pershore has never mentioned the matter to me since.'

'Do you remember the registration number of the car, Mr Sulgrave?'

'Not off-hand, but if you care to ring me up at the showrooms tomorrow, I can tell you.'

'I'll come and see you there. I want some particulars of the pressure valve that forms part of your new transmission.'

George glanced at him curiously. 'Do you?' he said. 'I wonder what it is about that valve that interests unlikely people. There was a queer old boy on the stand last night, after the show had closed, cross-examining me about it.'

Hanslet smiled. 'I think I know that queer old boy,' he replied. 'Good-afternoon, Mr Sulgrave. We'll meet again in the morning.'

CHAPTER XIII

'And that's that,' Hanslet concluded. 'I couldn't bounce a full confession out of Bryant. Not that that worries me much. He'll give himself away, sooner or later. That type of murderer always does.'

He was sitting in Dr Priestley's study that same Sunday evening, and had just recounted his adventures of the day. His host had listened to him closely, and seemed to display a greater interest in the case than he had hitherto done. But the assured tone of the superintendent's last remark seemed to displease him. 'And if Bryant does not give himself away, as you so confidently expect, what then?' he asked sharply.

'Oh, I'll run him to earth all right,' Hanslet replied. 'It's only a matter of patience, after all. Lots of people must have seen him at Olympia on Monday. Some of them would recognise him if they were confronted with him. And eventually I shall run to earth somebody who saw him carrying something heavy and bulky. Perhaps he was even seen to walk to the Solent stand. It will be my job to keep on until I get the evidence I want. Weary work, I grant you.'

'You are convinced that this evidence exists?' Dr Priestley asked.

'It must exist. This is a cut and dried case. We know the identity of the murderer, and the means he adopted. It's only a matter of getting corroborative evidence which will convince a jury. And, with so many people about at the time, it's a certainty that this evidence will be forthcoming.'

Dr Priestley shook his head. 'The presumption that Bryant killed his uncle is very strong, I admit,' he said. 'But upon what grounds do you treat it as a foregone conclusion?'

Hanslet shrugged his shoulders. 'I know your methods pretty well by now, Professor,' he replied. 'If somebody puts a drawing-pin point upwards in my chair, and I sit on it, I know immediately what has happened. But not you. You would extract the drawing-pin from your anatomy and examine it for traces of blood before you would be satisfied. Isn't that so?'

Dr Priestley smiled. 'All first impressions require to be verified before they can be classed as correct,' he replied.

'This isn't a matter of first impressions. Here's a man who admits having tried to murder another by poisoning him with carbon monoxide. His motive for doing so is evident. On the very next day his intended victim dies by another means. The person is proved to have been in the vicinity at the time. What further proof of his guilt could you possibly want?'

'I say that those facts do not amount to proof, however suggestive they may be. May I point out that the same line of argument might be adopted in the case of at least one other individual? Hardisen admits having shot at Pershore. Two days later Pershore dies at the Motor Show. A method by which he might have been killed has been demonstrated, but we have no knowledge that this method was actually employed. Hardisen says he was at Olympia at the time, but so far there is no proof that this statement is correct. He was on bad terms with Pershore. Does it therefore follow that he is guilty of Pershore's murder?'

Hanslet shifted impatiently in his chair. 'That's logic, I suppose,' he replied. 'But a comparison of motive is enough. What had Hardisen to gain by Pershore's death? Nothing, beyond the gratification of a ridiculous grudge. Bryant, on the other hand, stood to gain what may turn out to be a very considerable sum.'

'Apparent motive is apt to be misleading,' Dr Priestley said quietly. 'I believe that Pershore was murdered, but that the motive which inspired his murder has not yet been approached. Let us put prejudice aside for the moment, and treat the murderer as an unknown person. We will assume that he killed his victim by a blow with the pressure valve. The first question we must ask ourselves is this. Was his action premeditated, or did he, on a sudden impulse, avail himself of an opportunity which presented itself?'

Hanslet smiled. He was quite ready to humour the professor. 'The fact that two, if not three previous attempts had been made, rather suggests premeditation, doesn't it?' he replied.

'Very well. Let us see what the theory of premeditation involves. First, a knowledge on the part of the murderer that Pershore intended to visit the Motor Show on Monday. Who could have had this knowledge? Pershore was not a person who could have been expected to visit the Show, and he appears to have kept his intention secret.'

'Hardisen couldn't have known, anyhow. On the other hand, we only have Bryant's word for it that his uncle didn't tell him on the previous day.'

'If Bryant had intended to murder his uncle at Olympia on Monday, it is highly improbable that he would have announced publicly in advance that he intended to visit the Motor Show that day. We will pass on to the next point. The murderer must have made his plans in advance. He must have been aware of the conditions existing upon Stand 1001. He must have known that the pressure valve was available, and noted its suitability to his purpose. He must, therefore, have made a previous visit to Olympia.'

'I'll make it my business to find out if Bryant did so, Professor. Now you mention it, I remember that Hardisen said he had been to the Show on the previous Saturday afternoon.'

Dr Priestley shook his head. 'I do not want you to limit the identity of the murderer,' he said. 'You do so because both have confessed to what we may call the infliction of bodily harm upon Pershore. The wounding and the poisoning by carbon monoxide are thus accounted for. But is the poisoning by arsenic yet fully explained?'

'We know the source of the poison. But I'll admit that I'm not satisfied how the olives found their way into the cupboard in Pershore's study. I'm inclined to think that Bryant knows nothing about it. Anyway, I'm prepared to give him the benefit of the doubt for the moment. But there's always Mrs Bryant to be considered.'

'When do you think the olives were put in the cupboard?'

'Judging by the amount of arsenic found in the body, I

do not see how they can have been put there later than Friday the fifth.'

'When did Bryant receive the cable informing him of Micah Pershore's death?'

'About five o'clock on that same afternoon.'

'Then Bryant, or Mrs Bryant, had very little time in which to act. They had to procure both the arsenic and the olives. The insertion of the poison in each individual olive must have occupied a considerable time. An opportunity had then to be found to convey the prepared olives to Firlands, and to insert them in the cupboard. This being so, I think it extremely unlikely that the Bryants had any part in this particular attempt. They had no motive for the murder of Pershore before their reception of the cable from the Argentine. I am convinced that another motive already existed. That, in fact, the murderer of Pershore had determined upon the crime long before Friday the fifth.'

'Well, then, we come back to Miss Rissington, with Hardisen as her accomplice. She had the motive. And now there's that queer business about the car which Pershore bought for her, and of which she had said nothing.'

'That car will, I think, prove to be a clue of the first importance,' said Dr Priestley. 'But we will discuss that later. For the moment, let me put this suggestion before you. In all, there were three attempts to inflict bodily harm on Pershore. Two of them have now been explained. The perpetrator of the third is as yet unknown. I believe that this case is remarkable, in that three separate agencies, each inspired by a different motive, were simultaneously antagonistic to Pershore. We do not yet know the identity of the third agent, nor the motive which inspired him. But it is not impossible that the agent who attempted to murder

Pershore by means of the olives was responsible for his death at Olympia.'

'But that's just what I have been arguing all along, Professor!' Hanslet exclaimed.

'Yes. But your search for the third agent is limited by the motives already apparent. The Bryants and Miss Rissington have pecuniary motives. Hardisen was suffering under a sense of injury. But what if some far more powerful motive existed, the nature of which has not yet been realised?'

'Well, if it did exist, all I can say is that it has been most carefully concealed.'

'No doubt. When a man has grounds for jealousy, he does not usually advertise the fact.'

'Jealousy!' Hanslet exclaimed. 'Who on earth can have been jealous of Pershore, and why?'

'I dare say that Mrs Markle could tell us that,' Dr Priestley replied. 'But perhaps we can deduce the grounds of jealousy for ourselves. Let us endeavour to piece together the various scraps of information in our possession.

'You will remember, no doubt, the rather vague hints thrown out by Miss Rissington's aunt, Mrs Capel. In themselves, they were of no significance. She merely suggested to you that Pershore's morals were not beyond reproach. You did not press her for details, considering the matter of no importance to your inquiry. It is very doubtful whether she could have given you any further information. She was probably relying upon her feminine intuition. But, all the same, her remarks were suggestive.

'Then we come to the internal arrangements at Firlands, which you have described to me. Pershore had so arranged matters that he could receive visitors in his study without the knowledge of his household. The access to the garden from the lane, and the side door close to the study were convenient. He improved matters by fitting the baize door at the end of the passage, and forbidding anybody to pass that door except upon his express invitation.

'Next, the discovery by the parlourmaid of the lace-edged handkerchief in the study. Appearances already suggested that he received visitors there secretly. The handkerchief provided the further suggestion that these visitors were, at least occasionally, of the female sex.

'But most significant of all are the events of Saturday evening. These, on the face of them, are utterly inexplicable. Let us examine them dispassionately. Hardisen fires at Pershore and wounds him. Pershore exhibits neither surprise nor resentment. He gives Mrs Markle an obviously false explanation of the noise which he has heard. He does his best to conceal what has happened, and subsequently destroys the blood-stained garments. He is, quite obviously, desperately anxious to hide the fact that he has been wounded.

'Nor is he alone in wishing to keep the incident a profound secret. There is a witness to it, a woman. Her actions are as inexplicable as Pershore's. She drives off at once, without making any attempt to inform the police that an armed man of homicidal tendencies is at large in the lane. She limits her activities to telephoning to Firlands, and inquiring after Pershore's health, refusing to give her name.

'Now, it appears to me that there is only one rational explanation of these extraordinary facts. This woman was in the habit of visiting Firlands, and of concealing her visits from some third person, possibly her husband. When the shot is fired, both she and Pershore, conscience-stricken, jump to the same conclusion. The armed man could be no other than this third person, who has discovered the intrigue.

'You see now why each of them acted as they did. They were bound to keep silence, or the relationship between them would be exposed. Pershore dare not confront the injured party. The woman's instinct would be to get home as soon as possible, in the hope that she had not been definitely recognised, and could deny her presence at Firlands. It would be interesting to know what her feelings were when she discovered that the aggressor was not the person she expected.'

Hanslet considered this with a puzzled frown. 'I thought at first that the woman was Mrs Bryant,' he said. 'Until Bryant told me about that summons, that is. I checked that up, and found it was correct. Her car was certainly standing outside the theatre at nine o'clock on Saturday evening. So I came to the conclusion that it couldn't have been her. And now I hear about this other car, exactly like hers. So it may have been her, after all.'

Dr Priestley frowned at this inconsequent speech. 'That is not very clear reasoning,' he replied. 'But I think there is good reason to believe that the woman seen by Hardisen was not Mrs Bryant.

'Consider the curious statements made by Sulgrave, concerning Pershore's purchase of a car. I am assuming that you will be able to verify these statements tomorrow. The only condition made by the purchaser was that it should be exactly like Bryant's. It might be argued that he liked Bryant's car, and wished his niece to possess one like it. But I think that, in fact, he had another reason entirely.

'Pershore told Sulgrave that the car was intended as a birthday present for Miss Rissington. Her birthday is past, and there is no evidence that she ever received the car. It seems probable, therefore, that it was intended for some other person, whose identity Pershore did not wish to reveal.

'As I have already explained, there is reason to believe that Pershore was engaged in an intrigue with a woman, who was in the habit of visiting Firlands secretly. The car was purchased, in all probability, in order to enable her to do so without arousing attention. This car, exactly similar to Bryant's, would be mistaken for his by anyone seeing it in the vicinity of Firlands. I think we may say, with practical certainty, that this was the car seen by Hardisen on Saturday evening.'

'Well, if I can get the necessary particulars from Sulgrave in the morning, it oughtn't to be very difficult to trace it.'

Dr Priestley smiled. 'If you can do that, you should find the answer to many questions,' he replied. 'These questions are as follows. Who prepared the poisoned olives? How, and by what agency, were they placed in Pershore's study? What was the true reason for Pershore's visit to the Motor Show? And, finally, was he murdered there, and if so, by whom?'

The superintendent looked puzzled. 'I don't see how tracing that car is going to answer all those questions,' he said.

Dr Priestley made an impatient gesture. 'Then, when you have traced it, you had better consult me again,' he said. 'You will forgive me if I point out that it is already eleven o'clock, and that I like to go to bed as early as possible on Sunday evenings?'

So Hanslet said good-night, and left the house. He began his search early the next morning by a visit to the Comet showrooms. Here he obtained full particulars of the car which Pershore had bought, and sent out an army of subordinates to make inquiries. By nine o'clock that evening he was once more in Dr Priestley's study, triumphant, and eager to make his report.

'I've traced that car, Professor,' he said. 'And, as I suspected it would, the trail led me straight back to Philip Bryant. If you meant what you said last night, that the discovery of the car answers all those questions, I've got him by the short hairs.'

'Bryant!' exclaimed Dr Priestley. 'I certainly did not expect that he would be involved. Perhaps you will give me further details?'

'Oh, it was simple enough. I got the registered number of the car from Sulgrave, GW 4229. That's a London number, and I applied to the registration authorities. They confirmed that this number had been issued in respect of a Comet saloon car, painted blue, the property of Nahum Pershore, of Firlands, Weybridge.

'Then I sent men round the garages and second-hand shops to look for it. I thought that perhaps, now Pershore was dead, the car might have been put up for sale. And I was right. It was found in the Euston Road, in charge of Bradshaw and Co., second-hand dealers. As soon as I heard this, I went to the place and got the whole story.

'The car had been brought to them last Tuesday, the day after Pershore's death, by a gentleman who said he wished to sell it. He produced the registration book and the certificate of insurance. I saw these, and found that they were both in the name of Nahum Pershore.

'The man who brought the car explained that the owner was dead, and that he represented his executors. A figure was agreed upon, and the firm promised to do their best to sell the car at a price not less than this. It was also arranged that written confirmation of this should come from the executors. The man then cleared out, and nothing has been seen of him since. Nor has anything in the way of confirmation been received from Pershore's executors.'

'But surely Bradshaw and Co. asked the man who brought the car for his name?' Dr Priestley asked.

'They did. And he gave it to them. Philip Bryant, of Firlands, Weybridge. Now what about it, Professor?'

For some moments Dr Priestley made no reply. And then a queer smile hovered for a moment at the corners of his mouth. 'Have you mentioned your discovery to Bryant?' he asked.

'Not yet. I wanted to see you first. You promised to explain how those questions would be answered, you know.'

'Yes, when you had performed your part. At present, I do not consider that the car has been adequately traced.'

'Traced! Why, I'll show it to you, if you like to come to the Euston Road tomorrow. There's no doubt about the identity of the car. I've looked at the engine and chassis numbers, and they agree with those given me by Sulgrave, and with those entered in the registration book.'

'I do not doubt the identity of the car,' said Dr Priestley. 'But its present whereabouts are of no great importance. Where was it kept prior to Tuesday last?'

Hanslet shrugged his shoulders. 'I'll very soon find that out,' he replied. 'Bryant will have to explain how he came into possession of it. If you've nothing more to tell me, I'll go around to his flat and see him now.'

Dr Priestley raised no objection to this, and Hanslet departed. When he had gone, Dr Priestley gave Harold certain detailed instructions. 'My deductions may be at fault, but I think not,' he concluded. 'If you are successful, telephone at once to me and to Superintendent Hanslet. You had better set to work directly after breakfast tomorrow.'

CHAPTER XIV

Shortly before noon next day, Dr Priestley was summoned to the telephone. Harold spoke to him, and his tone was jubilant. 'I've found out where the car was kept, sir. In a garage here at Surbiton. I have already rung up the superintendent, and he will come down by the train which leaves Waterloo at 12.50. He will look out for you there.'

'Well done, my boy!' Dr Priestley replied. 'I will travel down by the same train. You had better meet us at Surbiton station.'

He met Hanslet on the platform, shortly before the train started, and the two entered a compartment which they had to themselves. The superintendent was obviously puzzled. 'Merefield rang me up, and said he had found out that this confounded car used to be kept in a garage in Surbiton,' he said. 'I suppose that you're behind this, Professor?'

'Yes. I thought that Surbiton was the most likely place in which to look for it,' Dr Priestley replied. 'What explanation had Bryant to give of the affair?'

'He refused to give any explanation. Swore that he knew nothing about the car, and that he had never heard of Bradshaw and Co. And it looks as if he were telling the truth. He offered to go with me to the Euston Road early this morning. The people there were positive that he was not the man who brought them the car for sale.'

'That is very much what I expected. In fact, I was convinced that this man was not Bryant. You will observe, however, that he was sufficiently aware of Mr Pershore's affairs to know whom he had appointed as his executors.'

'That's all very well, Professor,' replied Hanslet impatiently. 'But where does this mysterious woman of yours come in?'

'That we shall probably learn when we reach Surbiton,' said Dr Priestley. 'Until then, it will be useless to indulge in conjecture.'

He refused to say any more, and they completed their journey in silence. Harold met them at Surbiton station, and led them to a garage a short distance away. Here Hanslet introduced himself to the proprietor. 'I'm told that you know something about a car I'm looking for,' he said. 'A small Comet saloon, painted blue, registered number GW 4229.'

'You're just a week too late, I'm afraid, superintendent,' the garage proprietor replied. 'The car was driven away from here last Tuesday, and I haven't seen it since.'

'Who drove it away?'

'The lady who always drove it. Miss Rissington, her name is.'

This answer was so wholly unexpected that Hanslet could only stare at the man in amazement. The car had been bought for Miss Rissington, then, after all. But she had been in Paris on the previous Tuesday! Or was her alleged visit to Paris merely a carefully planned alibi, arranged between her, Mrs Sulgrave, and Hardisen? Instead of growing clearer, the plot seemed to thicken.

'You say that Miss Rissington was the regular driver of the car,' said Hanslet. 'When did it first come into your charge?'

'Last June. A lady came in here and said that her name was Miss Rissington, and that she lived with her brother in Surbiton. Her uncle, Mr Pershore, who lived at Weybridge, had bought a car, and she was to drive it for him. She asked if we would garage the car for her, and we agreed. She then gave us a written authorisation from Mr Pershore, for us to collect the car from the Comet showrooms. We did so, and kept it here until last Tuesday. Miss Rissington took the car out frequently, and settled our account for garage, petrol, and so on monthly, in cash.'

'Did you ever see her uncle, Mr Pershore?'

'We never saw anybody but Miss Rissington. She was always alone when she took the car out and brought it back. We understood that she picked up her uncle at Weybridge and dropped him there.'

'What explanation did she give when she took the car away last Tuesday?'

'She was in mourning, and told us that her uncle was dead. She and her brother were going to stay at Weybridge for a few days, over the funeral, and they would garage the car there until the executors had decided what was to be done with it.'

Having elicited this information, they left the garage. 'I can't make head or tail of this,' exclaimed Hanslet peevishly, as soon as they were outside. 'There's only one thing to do, and that is to take the next train to Weybridge and see what Miss Rissington has to say for herself.'

'I should not be in too great a hurry,' replied Dr Priestley. 'Let me see. You said, I think, that Mr and Mrs Chantley live in Surbiton? Mr Chantley will be at his office, I expect. But we might find Mrs Chantley at home.'

'Mrs Chantley!' Hanslet exclaimed. 'What on earth do you want to see her about?'

'She was at one time a friend of Miss Rissington's. And, since she lives in Surbiton, she may possibly be able to tell us why Miss Rissington garaged the car here.'

Hanslet did not seem very struck by the idea. But, in the end, he yielded to Dr Priestley's quiet insistence. They made their way to the Chantleys' house, Harold being told to await them.

Mrs Chantley had just finished lunch, and received them in the drawing-room. She looked pale and ill under her make-up, and glanced from one to the other nervously. It was left to Hanslet to begin the conversation.

'I called upon your husband a day or two ago,' he said pleasantly. 'I had not then the pleasure of making your acquaintance, Mrs Chantley. I am wondering now if you can help me. You were, at one time, on friendly terms with Miss Rissington, were you not?'

At this question a look, almost that of a hunted animal, came into her eyes. 'Well, yes, Betty Rissington and I were quite friendly once,' she replied. 'But I haven't seen anything of her for months, you know. She has deliberately avoided me.'

'This avoidance began about last June, did it not?' asked Dr Priestley quietly.

Until now Mrs Chantley's eyes had been fixed upon the

superintendent. She seemed half afraid of his imposing bulk and stern inquiring features. Now she turned to this undistinguished elderly gentleman, whose expression was masked by his spectacles. Whoever he might be, his appearance was not alarming. She relaxed into a faint smile.

'Yes, I think it was about June,' she replied.

Dr Priestley nodded. 'I thought so,' he said. 'Then perhaps you are not aware that about that time her uncle, Mr Pershore, bought a car for her to drive, and that she kept it at a garage in this town?'

A look of utter horror came into Mrs Chantley's eyes. She stiffened, and stared at Dr Priestley as though at some ghastly apparition. And when she found words, they were slow and hesitating, as though her lips found difficulty in forming them. 'A car for Betty? Yes, I did hear something about it. But I don't know anything for certain.'

'Oh, I think you do, Mrs Chantley,' Dr Priestley replied. And then, with a sudden change of manner, 'You must have been greatly relieved when you learnt that Mr Pershore had not been seriously injured by the shot which was fired at him.'

She stared at him for an instant as though petrified. And then, with a sudden gesture, she hid her face in her hands, and burst into tears.

Hanslet uttered a queer sound, something between a growl and an exclamation of astonishment. But Dr Priestley leant forward and touched her gently on the shoulder.

'There is nothing to be afraid of,' he said soothingly. 'I am fully aware of the affection that existed between you and Mr Pershore. You are naturally very much upset by his death. And I am sure that you will only be too anxious to help us to clear up the mystery which surrounds it.'

She nodded, but without looking up. And Dr Priestley continued. 'You saw a good deal of Mr Pershore. You used to meet him in London, and he bought you a car, so that you could drive over to Weybridge and meet him at Firlands. It was his suggestion that you should keep the car in a garage here, and give your name as Miss Rissington. I think that is correct, is it not?'

She looked up, with a foolish expression of surprise on her tear-stained face. 'Yes, that's right,' she replied. 'But I can't think how you found out. Nobody but us knew anything about it. Nahum and I were always very careful.'

'I'm sure you were. Now, the last time you drove to Firlands was on the Saturday before Mr Pershore's death. Was he expecting you?'

'Not exactly, though I told him I would run over then if I could. I only went to give him a message. I wasn't there more than a few minutes.'

'You drove over after dinner. Ah, yes, and perhaps you had a key to the door leading from the garden into the lane?'

'Yes. Nahum gave me one at the time he bought the car. I used to let myself in, walk up the garden, and tap at the study window.'

'I see. Now, would you mind telling me what the message was that you had for him?'

'It was about going to the Motor Show. I had asked Nahum to take me one afternoon, and he had promised to do so. But the difficulty was to fix the day. My husband had told me that he wanted to go one afternoon, and, of course, Nahum and I didn't want him to see us together there. And I couldn't find out from him what day he meant to go.

'But at dinner on Saturday my husband told me that he had a business appointment which would take him out of London on Monday, and that he might not be home that night. I thought that this would be the chance for Nahum and me to go to the Show. After dinner my husband went out to play bridge, as he very often does, and I got the car and went over to Firlands to tell Nahum about it. And as I was coming away . . .' She broke off, and shuddered.

'As you were coming away, you saw a man with a gun, and heard a shot fired,' said Dr Priestley. 'You did not recognise the man in the dark, but you thought it was your husband, who had laid a trap for you and Mr Pershore. You drove straight back here and telephoned to Firlands?'

She looked at him wonderingly. 'Yes. I didn't know what to do. I had to find out what had happened, or I should have gone mad. Nahum had told me never to ring him up, in case somebody else answered the telephone and recognised my voice. But I simply had to risk it, that time.'

'And you never discovered who fired the shot?'

'No. It wasn't my husband. And that was all I cared about, since Nahum wasn't hurt. Mrs Markle told me that. When my husband came home that night, he brought one of his friends with him, for a drink, and I knew from what they said that he had been playing bridge in a house not far from here, all the time.'

'That must have been a great relief to you, Mrs Chantley. Now, to proceed to the following Monday. Did you keep your appointment with Mr Pershore?'

'No, I didn't. This is what happened. I had arranged to meet Nahum at the Addison Road entrance to Olympia at twelve o'clock, and lunch with him there. But just as I was going to start, my husband rang up from his office, and told me that his business appointment had fallen through, and that he was going to the Motor Show instead. He asked me if I would like to meet him there, but I told him that I couldn't, as I had some calls to pay. I rang up Nahum at his office, but he wasn't there, and I didn't know where to catch him. So I thought it safest not to go to Olympia at all, and to explain why later.'

Dr Priestley glanced at Hanslet, who was listening wide-eyed to this conversation. 'Now, Mrs Chantley, you have told me that you saw Mr Pershore on Saturday evening,' he said. 'Had you seen him previously that week?'

'Oh, yes, several times. I spent an hour or so with him in his study on Friday evening, after dinner, when my husband had gone out.'

Dr Priestley nodded. 'Yes, I thought that was probably the case. And you took him a bottle of olives, knowing that he ate one every night, did you not?'

'Why, how can you possibly have known that?' she exclaimed. 'Yes, I took him some olives that evening. I often used to. Mrs Markle used to keep him supplied, but I liked him to have the ones I brought him. So did he. He always said they tasted better.'

'Where did you get the olives, Mrs Chantley?'

'Oh, from the grocer I always deal with. I always kept a bottle or two in my bedroom so that there would be one ready for me to give Nahum when he wanted it.'

Hanslet had been fidgeting restlessly ever since the olives had been mentioned. He was on the point of interjecting a remark, but Dr Priestley quelled him with an almost savage look. 'You took Mr Pershore a bottle of olives, Mrs Chantley,' he said. 'Did you notice anything peculiar about it?'

'No, I don't think so. It seemed just the same as usual. Oh, now I come to think of it, I remember that this one wasn't wrapped up in paper, as they usually are.'

'What became of the bottle of olives which was already in the cupboard in Mr Pershore's study?'

'Oh, Nahum and I ate those, and I brought the empty bottle back with me, so that the servants at Firlands shouldn't find it. Then we opened the bottle that I had brought. Nahum said we had better take out two or three, so that it would look just like the bottle that was there before. But neither of us could eat any more, so we threw them in the fire. I remember that they burnt with a funny smell, almost like garlic.'

Dr Priestley got up and strolled across to the window. 'Your garden is in excellent condition, Mrs Chantley,' he said. 'It is in great contrast to the garden at Firlands. But perhaps, unlike Mr Pershore, you are interested in gardening?'

'Oh, it's my husband's hobby, not mine,' she replied.

'Indeed? A very exacting hobby. There is always something to be done in a garden. Those gravel paths, for instance, are most beautifully kept. Your husband must spend a considerable amount of time in weeding them?'

'Oh, he uses a weed-killer. I know that, for he asked me to get him some a few weeks ago, and I had to sign my name in a book when I bought it.'

Dr Priestley turned from the window and sat down again. 'By the way, Mrs Chantley, what became of the car that Mr Pershore bought for your use?'

'I don't know. My husband sent it to Nahum's executors, I believe.'

'Your husband!' Dr Priestley exclaimed. 'How did he learn of its existence?'

'I wish I knew!' she replied. 'I was utterly amazed when he spoke of it. But he's like that. You never can tell what he knows and what he doesn't. It happened on the Tuesday after Nahum's death. My husband came home to lunch, a thing he very rarely does. And then he told me, quite casually, that he had heard at the office that Nahum was dead. He was quite nice about it, and said that he knew I should be sorry, as I had kept up my friendship for him, even though they had quarrelled.

'I was never more astonished in my life, for I had no idea that he knew anything about my seeing Nahum. Even the shock of hearing of his death was nothing to that, at least not at the moment. I asked him what he meant, and he told me that he knew all about the car. But he seemed to think that Nahum had bought it for me to drive him about in. He didn't know anything about my going over to Firlands in it.' A sudden look of horror came into her face. 'Oh, and you won't tell him anything, will you?' she added pleadingly.

'No, I shall not tell him,' Dr Priestley replied. 'And I think I can promise that the superintendent will not do so either. Your husband undertook the disposal of the car?'

'Yes. He said that now Nahum was dead, it must be returned to his executors. But I must not appear in the matter. It would never do for Betty Rissington or the Bryants to know that I had been driving Nahum about. They might say spiteful things. Fortunately, the car was in his name. It could be disposed of without any questions being asked, and my husband told me that he had made arrangements for doing so. I was to fetch the car, and drive it to the top of Putney Hill, where a man from the office would meet me and take it over. He wouldn't tell me any more. I did what he told me, and that's all I know about it.'

'What time are you expecting your husband home this evening, Mrs Chantley?'

'Oh, he's usually home by six.'

'Is the garage where you kept the car far from here?'

'Not very far. About five or ten minutes walk.'

'I wonder if you would mind showing it to me?'

'I will if you like,' she replied rather doubtfully. 'But you won't tell them who I really am, will you? It was Nahum's idea that I should tell them that I was his niece, Betty Rissington.'

'No, I will tell them nothing,' Dr Priestley replied.

'Well, then, I will go and put on a hat. I won't keep you a moment.' She rose to leave the room, and Hanslet sprang up to open the door for her. 'What's the game, Professor?' he whispered, as soon as he heard her footsteps ascending the stairs.

'This!' replied Dr Priestley urgently. 'We must make it impossible for her to communicate with her husband. That is why I am anxious to get her out of the house. While I am walking with her to the garage and back, you must communicate with the telephone exchange and see that the line is put out of order. Then we must watch this house and the post office, in case she attempts to send a telegram. Hush! Here she comes.'

Dr Priestley seemed that afternoon to have lost much of his wonted activity. He managed to spin out his walk with Mrs Chantley until it occupied nearly half an hour. His companion was consumed with curiosity. She made many tentative endeavours to draw Dr Priestley, without any success. Until at last she was forced to put the matter bluntly. 'I can't understand how you came to know all about—about Nahum and me,' she said. 'You must be a friend of his, of course. It's odd that he should never have mentioned you to me.'

'I was not acquainted with Mr Pershore,' Dr Priestley replied. 'But you may rest assured that I did not learn your secret from any other human being.'

And with this cryptic remark Mrs Chantley was forced to be content.

Dr Priestley escorted her to her house, where Hanslet rejoined them. They then left together, and walked away. 'She won't be able to get in touch with her husband. I've seen to that,' said Hanslet. 'I've asked the local people to keep an eye on the house. Suppose we find a decent place to get something to eat? I'm famished.'

They picked up Harold, and then entered a quiet tea-shop, choosing a table where they could talk without being overheard. And then Hanslet took steps to satisfy his curiosity. 'Whatever made you tumble to the fact that Mrs Chantley was the woman in the case, Professor?' he asked.

'It was not very difficult to do so,' Dr Priestley replied. 'The Chantleys, from the first moment that their name was mentioned, seemed worth bearing in mind. Mrs Markle, as you told me, was reluctant to discuss them. She was surprised when they attended the funeral, but could give no very convincing reason for her surprise. How much she knows it is difficult to say. But I should not be surprised to learn that she had some inkling of Mrs Chantley's clandestine visits to Firlands.

'At first, of course, I merely wondered what could be the reason for Mrs Markle's reticence. She seemed willing enough to talk about any other subject. It was not until you described to me your conversation with Chantley that my suspicions were aroused. He expressed a dislike for gossip, but, in spite of this, he poured out a flood of intimate personal details, involving Mr Pershore, his household, his friends and relations. It struck me then that he must know more about the case than he was willing to reveal.

'The line he took with you was very clever. He did not know what you had already discovered from other sources. It was probable that you knew that some woman was in the habit of visiting Firlands, but that you were not aware of her identity. His object was to arouse the suspicion in your mind that she was Mrs Bryant.

'There was another curious point about his conversation. He could not have learnt of the poisoned olives or the substituted inhalant from any external source. And yet, without any prompting on your part, he suggested a reason for Mrs Markle wishing to revenge herself upon her employer. This made me wonder whether he knew that the house contained evidence of attempts upon Pershore's life. If he did know this, it would only be because he had been concerned in one at least of those attempts.

'The next step was to examine his possible motive. He had, apparently, nothing to gain by Pershore's death. On the other hand, one of the most powerful motives for murder is jealousy. This caused me to believe that a possibility existed that the woman seen by Hardisen was Mrs Chantley.

'The car bought by Mr Pershore was the next clue. As I told you when you first mentioned it, I saw at once the probable use that had been made of it. The curious circumstances surrounding its disposal confirmed me in my belief.

The woman, or the jealous party, would naturally be anxious to get rid of it, since, being registered in Pershore's name, it was a clue connecting the woman with him.

'The method adopted by Chantley of nullifying this clue was sufficiently ingenious. Once the car had been left at Bradshaw's, only the most exhaustive inquiries could have traced it back to the garage here. And then it would have been learnt that it was in the name of Miss Rissington. This would not have helped your investigations, but would have presented you with a fresh puzzle which you might have found considerable difficulty in solving.'

'You're right there, Professor,' said Hanslet. 'How did you trace the car back, though?'

'I did not trace it. I deduced where it might have been kept. The car had been bought to provide a means whereby a certain woman might visit Firlands. Of that I felt fairly certain. If that woman were Mrs Chantley, it was reasonable to suppose that the car had been kept at Surbiton. Quite obviously, she could not keep it at her own house. The most probable alternative seemed to be a public garage. I sent Harold down here this morning to make inquiries, and the result proved the correctness of my deduction.'

Hanslet nodded. 'Yes, it's simple enough,' he said. 'I might have thought of it myself. And you were quite right. The discovery of the car has answered those questions of yours. We know now why Pershore went to the Motor Show. Not to look at the cars, but because he expected to meet Mrs Chantley there. And we know how the poisoned olives got into Pershore's study. But we don't know yet for certain who poisoned them. And I don't know how you guessed the part that Mrs Chantley played.'

'It was hardly guesswork. You were not satisfied with

the evidence that any of the other persons in the case had put the olives in the cupboard. Eliminating them, my attention became fixed upon the woman seen by Hardisen. The precautions taken by Pershore to secure his privacy convinced me that this was by no means her first visit to Firlands. It seemed probable that the poisoned olives had been deposited on Friday. If it could be proved that the woman had visited the house on that day, a presumption was created that she had brought the olives with her. Mrs Chantley, on being questioned, admitted the fact at once.'

'Yes, it's easy enough to get the facts if you know who to ask for them. But how are we going to get proof of who put the poison into them?'

'That should not present any insuperable difficulty,' Dr Priestley replied.

They killed time until half-past five, and then took up a position from which they could keep the Chantleys' house under observation. Shortly before six a man walked up to the gate and let himself in. 'That's Chantley!' Hanslet exclaimed.

'Then we will interview him at once,' replied Dr Priestley. They reached the front door a second or two after it had closed behind Chantley, and Hanslet knocked insistently upon it. Chantley himself opened it, and recognised the superintendent. 'Hullo!' he said. 'Have you come to pay me another visit? I'm delighted to see you, and your friend. Come along into the library.'

He led the way into that very comfortable room, in the centre of which was a wide flat desk. Chantley placed a couple of chairs on the farther side of it for his visitors, and sat down on the near side, facing them across the desk. He looked fixedly at them in turn. 'Well, gentlemen, what can I do for you?' he asked.

It was Dr Priestley who replied. 'When did you first discover that your wife was in the habit of visiting Mr Pershore?' he asked.

Chantley flushed angrily. 'What authority have you for asking impertinent questions?' he demanded.

'The presence of Superintendent Hanslet gives me sufficient authority. I gather that you are unwilling to answer my question. But I may say that I have evidence that you were aware of this intimacy some little time before Pershore's death.'

'Have you, indeed?' replied Chantley. 'And may I ask what this evidence is?'

'It consists of a bottle of olives, found in Mr Pershore's study, into which a quantity of arsenic has been introduced.'

In spite of Chantley's self-control, the colour left his face, turning his cheeks a greenish white. But his reply was bold enough. 'A bottle of olives?' he exclaimed. 'What nonsense are you talking?'

'You force me to a full explanation. You had discovered your wife's intimacy with Mr Pershore, and you determined to end this, and at the same time to be revenged upon him. You became aware that your wife was in the habit of taking him olives, which you knew, from your previous friendship with him, that he kept for his personal use. You had access to the olives before they were taken to Firlands, and you decided to use them as the instrument of your revenge.'

Chantley uttered a forced laugh. 'This is a magnificent fairy story,' he said. 'I don't quite see the point of it, since the evidence at the inquest shows that whatever Pershore died of it most certainly wasn't from eating olives.'

'Had he continued to eat those particular olives, death would undoubtedly have ensued. You had procured an arsenical weed killer. Having opened a bottle of the olives which you found in your wife's room, you injected some of the poison into each of them. Then you replaced the metal cap on the bottle, leaving no trace of it having been opened, beyond the trifling circumstance that you omitted to wrap it up in its original paper.

'Your wife took this bottle of olives to Mr Pershore on the Friday preceding his death. He probably ate one of them that night, and another on Sunday. An incident, beyond your control, prevented him from eating one on Saturday. The amount of poison contained in two olives did not constitute a fatal dose. But that hardly mattered, since you had already devised an alternative means of achieving your object.'

Chantley's assurance was steadily ebbing. It was apparent to him that this detailed accusation was not made without full proof to support it. There was a moment or two of strained silence, and then he spoke, addressing the superintendent.

'I don't know how your friend discovered all this,' he said. 'But it's no good denying it. I did find out that my wife used to go and see Pershore, and I decided to give them both a fright. I poisoned the olives, taking care to put only a small dose in each, so that he would have to take several before the poison began to take effect. I meant to wait until he got really ill, and then tell my wife what I had done, and why. They would have hushed the matter up, in their own interests. I certainly had no intention of letting things go as far as Pershore's death.'

Hanslet would have replied to this, but Dr Priestley

225

forestalled him. 'An ingenious move, Mr Chantley,' he said. 'By confessing to a crime which proved abortive, you think to avoid being charged with a crime which proved successful. As I say, an alternative means of accomplishing your object had occurred to you. And I think that the source of the suggestion is sufficiently obvious.'

He rose, and walked up to one of the bookcases which surrounded the room. From this he selected a stout volume and returned with it to his chair. 'Your library consists mainly of books dealing with travel and adventure, Mr Chantley,' he continued remorselessly. 'Yet I find among them a work dealing with an entirely different subject. How and when did you acquire this copy of the latest edition of Dixon Mann's *Forensic Medicine and Toxicology?*'

'That?' replied Chantley uneasily. 'Oh, a doctor friend of mine gave it to me, not long ago.'

'Indeed? Surely rather a curious gift to a layman. Hardly the type of literature which would appeal to your normal taste, I should have thought. But, under the peculiar circumstances in which you were situated, you must have found it very useful. The effects of arsenic, and the necessary dose to produce those effects, are very fully described. No doubt you consulted this book before you tampered with the olives?'

'Well, yes, I did,' replied Chantley sullenly. And then a bright idea struck him. 'You see, I wanted to be on the safe side. I didn't want to kill Pershore, only to frighten him.'

'Then you admit having consulted the book? Perhaps, even, you turned the pages and found a piece of information which impressed itself upon your memory. This, I suppose, was before you took pains to ensure that Mr

Pershore should attend the Motor Show alone last Monday week?'

'I?' exclaimed Chantley. 'How should I know that Pershore would go to the Motor Show? I hadn't spoken to him for months before his death.'

'You knew that he had arranged with your wife to meet her there. And you had learnt that certain loose pieces of metal were displayed upon the Comet stand. Mr Pershore would naturally visit that stand, since his friend, Mr Sulgrave, is an employee of the Comet firm. With that passage from the text-book in your mind, you saw a means of killing Mr Pershore more certainly than by arsenic, and with the probability that the crime would never be traced to you.'

Dr Priestley paused, but Chantley made no reply. He stared at him with wide open and horror-stricken eyes, and his hand moved furtively towards one of the drawers of the desk.

'You followed Mr Pershore to the Comet stand,' continued Dr Priestley. 'Being careful, of course, that he should not see you. You picked up one of the pressure-valves, and pretended to examine it. When a suitable opportunity occurred, you struck Mr Pershore with it in the pit of the stomach. In the confusion which resulted, you made your escape, disposing of the pressure-valve in one of the cars on the Solent stand. I think I have narrated the events correctly, have I not?'

There was a moment of tense silence. Then, with a sudden movement, Chantley wrenched open the drawer upon which his hand was laid. Hanslet leapt from his chair, and was about to hurl himself across the desk, but Dr Priestley rose at the same moment, and thrust him violently aside.

The moment's delay enabled Chantley to achieve his purpose. He snatched an automatic pistol from the drawer, and held it to his temple. There was a report, deafening in the confined space. The pistol clattered to the floor, and Chantley sat for an instant, an expression of bewilderment in his face. Then he slumped forward, until his head struck the desk in front of him.

Hanslet turned savagely upon Dr Priestley. 'Why did you get in my way?' he demanded. 'I saw what he was up to, and I could have stopped him.'

'Exactly,' Dr Priestley replied placidly. 'And what then? You would have arrested him on a charge of murder. But you forget one thing. Could you have proved to the satisfaction of a jury that he was the actual murderer of Mr Pershore? That he, among the thousands assembled at Olympia at the time, struck the fatal blow, even if you could prove that such a blow had, in fact, been struck? I think you could not.'

'Well, perhaps you're right,' said Hanslet, as he gazed reflectively at the motionless body. 'There's a hell of a difference between knowing a thing and being able to prove it.'

The murderer of Mr Pershore having thus died by his own hand, Hanslet did not press the minor charge against Philip Bryant. Micah Pershore was found to have left a fortune of several thousand pounds, which fell to Philip, as Nahum Pershore's residuary legatee. But his career was at an end. With his attempt to poison his uncle known to the police, he could not continue his practice as a solicitor. He sold his partnership and went abroad, where he and Mrs Bryant spend their time wandering restlessly from place to place, the shadow of the house at Weybridge always upon their minds.

Betty Rissington spends a good deal of her time with the Sulgraves at Byfleet. A frequent visitor to the house is the salesman employed by the Solent Motor Car Co., who returned the pressure-valve to George Sulgrave on the evening of Mr Pershore's death. Irene Sulgrave watches them with an indulgent eye.

Mrs Markle, in the enjoyment of her annuity, tried for some weeks the experiment of living in a cottage in the country. But the experience of having nothing to do threatened her with premature death. Mr Hardisen stepped in and offered her a position as his own housekeeper, which she accepted with alacrity.

Those familiar with automobile design will be aware that the rivals of Comet Cars Ltd have displayed a strange apathy. Not one of them has shown the slightest eagerness to adopt the Lovell transmission.

And, perhaps, on the whole, they are wise.

THE END

Also available

Death at Breakfast

John Rhode

'One always embarks on a John Rhode book with a great feeling of security. One knows that there will be a sound plot, a well-knit process of reasoning and a solidly satisfying solution with no loose ends or careless errors of fact.'
DOROTHY L. SAYERS in *THE SUNDAY TIMES*

Victor Harleston awoke with uncharacteristic optimism. Today he would be rich at last. Half an hour later, he gulped down his breakfast coffee and pitched to the floor, gasping and twitching. When the doctor arrived, he recognised instantly that it was a fatal case of poisoning and called in Scotland Yard.

Despite an almost complete absence of clues, the circumstances were so suspicious that Inspector Hanslet soon referred the evidence to his friend and mentor, Dr Lancelot Priestley, whose deductions revealed a diabolically ingenious murder that would require equally fiendish ingenuity to solve.

'Death at Breakfast *is full of John Rhode's specialties: a new and excellently ingenious method of murder, a good story, and a strong chain of deduction.*'
DAILY TELEGRAPH

Also available

Invisible Weapons

John Rhode

'John Rhode never lets you down. A carefully worked out plot, precise detection, with no logical flaws or jumping to conclusions, and enough of character and atmosphere to carry the thing along.'

FRANCIS ILES in the *DAILY TELEGRAPH*

The murder of old Mr Fransham while washing his hands in his niece's cloakroom was one of the most astounding problems that ever confronted Scotland Yard. Not only was there a policeman in the house at the time, but there was an ugly wound in the victim's forehead and nothing in the locked room that could have inflicted it.

The combined efforts of Superintendent Hanslet and Inspector Waghorn brought no answer and the case was dropped. It was only after another equally baffling murder had been committed that Dr Lancelot Priestley's orderly and imaginative deductions began to make the connections that would solve this extraordinary case.

'Any murder planned by Mr Rhode is bound to be ingenious.'

OBSERVER

Also available

Inspector French's
Greatest Case
Freeman Wills Crofts

At the offices of the Hatton Garden diamond merchant *Duke & Peabody*, the body of old Mr Gething is discovered beside a now-empty safe. With multiple suspects, the robbery and murder is clearly the work of a master criminal, and requires a master detective to solve it. Meticulous as ever, Inspector Joseph French of Scotland Yard embarks on an investigation that takes him from the streets of London to Holland, France and Spain, and finally to a ship bound for South America . . .

'Because he is so austerely realistic, Freeman Wills Croft is deservedly a first favourite with all who want a real puzzle.'
TIMES LITERARY SUPPLEMENT

Also available

Inspector French
and the Sea Mystery
Freeman Wills Crofts

Off the coast of Burry Port in south Wales, two fishermen discover a shipping crate and manage to haul it ashore. Inside is the decomposing body of a brutally murdered man. With nothing to indicate who he is or where it came from, the local police decide to call in Scotland Yard. Fortunately Inspector Joseph French does not believe in insoluble cases—there are always clues to be found if you know what to look for. Testing his theories with his accustomed thoroughness, French's ingenuity sets him off on another investigation . . .

'Inspector French is as near the real thing as any sleuth in fiction.'

SUNDAY TIMES

Also available

Inspector French
and the Box Office Murders
Freeman Wills Crofts

The suicide of a sales clerk at the box office of a London cinema leaves another girl in fear for her life. Persuaded to seek help from Scotland Yard, Miss Darke confides in Inspector Joseph French about a gambling scam by a mysterious trio of crooks and that she believes her friend was murdered. When the girl fails to turn up the next day, and the police later find her body, French's inquiries reveal that similar girls have also been murdered, all linked by their jobs and by a sinister stranger with a purple scar . . .

'Freeman Wills Crofts' crimes are solved with dogged diligence and attention to detail . . . they seem to have improved with age.'

INDEPENDENT

Also available

Inspector French and Sir John Magill's Last Journey
Freeman Wills Crofts

When Sir John Magill, the wealthy Irish industrialist, fails to show up at his home town on a well-publicised visit, neither his family nor the Belfast police can explain his disappearance. Foul play is suspected when his bloodstained hat is discovered, and Scotland Yard is called in. With his characteristic genius for reconstruction, Inspector French evolves a gruesome theory about what happened to the elderly man, but his reputation—and that of Scotland Yard—will depend on finding out who was responsible . . .

'Nobody takes more trouble to get every detail absolutely correct. This most workmanlike of sleuths unravels a really satisfying puzzle.'

DAILY MAIL